Revelation

A slave's voyage
of self-discovery

Part I of a Trilogy

Christopher Charlton

EmOhErotica
Leeds, UK

Published by EmOh Erotica, PO Box HP346, Leeds LS6 1UL, UK

British Library Cataloguing-in-Publication data: Chris Charlton

Revelation; a slave's voyage of self-discovery – the first part of a trilogy,

1. Title

ISBN   978-873031-33-9 (paperback)
          978-873031-34-6 (Kindle)

Cover design: Ben Matthews

TO
Paul and Wes

CONTENTS

Acknowledgements vi

The First Steps 7
Anticipation 15
Meeting... 27
Surprise 31
Peter's Discovery.. 43
Peter's inspection.. 52
Entering service 59
Learning.. 68
On trial.. 76
Morgan's surprise 85
Brian's support... 94
Sunday, Monday... 104
A long time in Spandex... 115
The Run 120
Cleansing.. 127
Preparation 134
Breakfast 141
Punishment 146
Ennui 153
The exercise 159
A role in life 172
Encouragement 178
Self-discipline.. 186

About the author... 194

ACKNOWLEDGEMENTS

I should like to thank Anthony, Dave, Jerry, Mark, Mark, Martin, Phil, Paul, Sam and Zac – who stimulated me and so later provided ideas and inspiration when my imagination had a chance to run free.

The First Steps

I knew what I was doing.

Or at least I thought I did. The listing had been quite clear.

SOUTH: 42, 6'2', 160 lbs, active, sadistic, dominant leatherman with well-equipped gamesroom will train willing obedient guys 25—45. Detailed application with full-length pic and previous training details.

It was nothing if not specific. It caught my attention and held it. The magazine stayed open at that page and none other as I jerked off yet again. I ringed it in red. Rarest – and best – of all, a phone number had been included.

It had taken me a while, but going through the phone book checking all the area codes had been worthwhile. The Master was only about sixty miles away. Should I call though? I was tempted. What could I be letting myself in for? It sounded so enticing. It was probably meant to. There weren't that many people around with playrooms. Early forties, a good age, and nicely-proportioned. I was however a little young. I was only twenty-two. I'd had experience though. And, it had never really been that satisfying. Somehow, this felt far more like the real thing. I wasn't sure why. It felt right. Yet, I was still nervous, reluctant.

Perhaps I should write. I didn't have a good full-length photograph that was for sure. And as for previous 'training details', they were sketchy to say the least. I knew what to do, and I thought that I did it reasonably well, but that I felt, came more from an innate need to serve or give pleasure than it did from training. I'd call. No, I'd write. I'd call. I'd write.

I can't remember how long it took me to call. This was the 1970s. We lived differently then. For one thing, no one had as many phones as we do nowadays. Ours was in the lobby. I'd have to call without any guarantee of privacy. At least, I thought, there was only one phone, so no one could eavesdrop on my conversation. Either my Mom or Dad could have walked through as I spoke. But, as the days went passed, I knew that I'd have to make that call. My choice was gradually, but steadily, receding. Destiny was encroaching. It had been nearly three years since I'd moved back to the family home. After being away at boarding school, rather than going straight on to college, I'd decided that I'd like a break. I'd found a job. The money wasn't great. It was expensive living in lodgings and running a small car, but I'd survived. Once, I'd even had enough left over to go to a leather store in the city and buy a harness. Another time, I'd bought a cock sheath with pinpricks on the inside. I'd enjoyed the relative freedom. Although I'd certainly had quite a lot of sex at school, and been introduced to some more 'esoteric' activities, it had been liberating to find other men in to leather and leathersex. Coming back to the family home had meant sacrificing some of that freedom. For the first year or so, it had been good. It was the longest time I'd spent close to my father since I'd been a child. But, thanks to my step-mother, the novelty was wearing off. It was to be thinking of moving on. I didn't know how, where, when or with whom, but I knew the time was approaching.

I also knew I had to be patient. Sex, especially hard sex, appealed and occasional evenings or nights away, even one night stands had some compensations. Father knew something was happening on such occasions, but he was sensible and wise enough not to ask any questions.

So, when an evening came when Mom was due to be out, I

decided that would be the evening I'd call. I'd got home from work around 6.30. I'd gone to my room to change out of my business suit and I'd pulled out the magazine and jerked off thinking about the ad. After eating, again I'd gone back to my room and jerked off again. It had taken slightly longer, but the orgasm had been equally intense. I tried to be casual after Mom had left. I can't remember what I'd been doing, but Dad had poured a beer and turned on the TV. Although I probably didn't need to say anything, now his attention was taken, I felt the need to check.

'Dad?' I asked.

'Yes?'

'I need to make a few calls. I don't want to be disturbed.'

'Sure,' he replied, half turning to me from his seat and giving me a knowing look.

'No problem,' he added. Take as long as you like. Your Mom's not in and the game starts soon.'

I went through to the lobby. I knew that I couldn't bring the magazine downstairs, so I'd copied the listing and the phone number into a note book. That had had the unexpected bonus of providing stimulation in the men's room at work several times in the last few days too.

Trying not to get too excited, I dialed the number. I held a pen in one hand and the phone in the other. I pressed my erection against the counter. It seemed ages before there was an answer.

'Yes.'

The voice on the other end was a deep southern American drawl. Wow! I hadn't been expecting that. I was surprised. It took me a moment to regain my senses.

'Good evening,' I said, speaking carefully, and as politely and respectfully as I could, before quietly adding, 'Sir .... Did you place a listing recently please?'

I waited. I hoped the number was right. At least, the phone hadn't been answered by a woman. There was a pause.

'Yes,' the husky voice said, 'I did.'

'Good, Sir,' I said, almost too quickly. 'I would like to apply for consideration please Sir ....'

'You sound young boy,' the voice said. 'You read what I said about age?'

'I did Sir,' I replied. 'I'm twenty-two; I hope that's not too young for you please Sir. I am keen, Sir.'

'You sound it, boy,' he said, before pausing again.

'Yes Sir,' I said, trying not to let the silence stop the conversation.

'Tell me about you, boy', he said.

'Well, Sir,' I began, 'I'm twenty-two, as I say Sir, and I have had some experience Sir, but I'd really like some more formal training Sir ....'

'Good boy.'

The drawl only heightened the man's sexiness. I suddenly felt that there was a determination, there was the strength, there was the knowledge that this was a man who knew what he wanted and knew how to get it.

'Thank you, Sir,' I said.

'Do you have a pen and paper there boy?'

'Yes, Sir.'

'Then take down this address, boy. I want you to write to me, telling me about you and your experience so far, boy. Is that clear?'

'Yes, Sir. That's clear, Sir.'

'Good boy.'

He gave me an address.

'Do you have a photograph boy?' he asked.

'Not a full length one, Sir,' I replied.

'Send me what you have boy. And you will go and write

that letter now, boy. And post it to me, first class first thing tomorrow boy.'

'Yes Sir. I'll do it straightaway Sir,' I said. My throat was getting dry.

'Good boy. You are not to touch your cock while you write, boy, is that clear?'

'Yes, Sir. That's clear, Sir.'

'Good. You will call me on Monday again, boy, at eight. Precisely.' That was just days away, merely enough time for him to get my letter.

'Yes, Sir.'

'Do you have a jockstrap boy?' he asked.

'Yes, Sir,' I replied.

'Then goodnight boy,' he said, putting the phone down.

The abruptness of the ending caught me a little by surprise. I'd expected, perhaps hoped for, something more, some politeness, some small talk, perhaps, but as I slowly put the phone down, I realized, accepted, that it was inappropriate.

Obedience, I thought, starts at once. He'd said don't touch my cock. He hadn't said anything else. I went and got a beer before returning to my room. I went to my typewriter and started work.

By the time I was finished, I was excited, but too tired to jerk off. And, I realized, while I had this man's address, I still didn't have his name.

It took a moment for the penny to drop, but I then knew that I didn't really need to know his name. He was a master, perhaps The Master; from the sound of his voice and the brief details I had, I could but hope. A name could even spoil it, I thought as I drifted off to sleep.

★ ★ ★

I was late to work the next day.

It had taken me longer than I expected to write the letter. I'd started several times, but it wasn't until I had torn up my fifth or sixth attempt that I'd accepted that I'd have to plan what I was going to write. It was 2am when I finally put the neatly-typed sheets into an envelope. Breakfast had been tense. Mom wanted to know why I'd been working so late. Despite Dad's pleas that the lad should be left alone, she'd continued her questioning.

'Look,' Dad finally said, 'he does write for a living. He had something to finish and got on with it. Now leave him alone.'

'He shouldn't stay up so long,' Mom nagged. 'Now he's going to be late.'

'I'll be OK,' I said.

Dad caught me a knowing look as I left, holding the envelope as I walked towards the car.

The traffic was heavy. It took me ages to find somewhere to park and only as I was walking towards the office did I realize that I only just had enough stamps for the heavy letter. Bills could wait. I knew where my priorities were. I crossed my fingers and kissed the seal on the back of the envelope before I dropped it into the mail box. I really hope this works out, I thought.

I was glad I was on call for work that weekend. It wasn't that busy, just a couple of calls to answer, but enough to provide the distraction I needed. So, I didn't have too much time to think about my letter and the unknown man with the deep sexy voice reading it. I didn't have too much time to think about the second call either, until nearer the time.

Monday would be different. Mom was home. Privacy would be even more difficult. Even trying to call dead on eight might be a problem. Certainly, I would have to talk quietly. Mother's hearing could be amazing, especially when she was suspicious. If she heard a 'Sir' she'd be quizzing me for hours.

Some interrogation scenes, I'd already discovered, could be fun. Others really could be torture.

After eating on the Monday, I'd gone to my room. I suspected that I should call as close to eight as I possibly could. I also knew that it was probably inviting least trouble if I left it to the last possible moment before running down the stairs to make a 'spontaneous' phone call.

Even then, as I helped Dad clear the dishes, I felt Mom was aware something was on my mind. For once, she knew better than to ask. At a minute to eight, I ran down the stairs, clutching my note book and pen.

I dialed the number. It was engaged. Shit, I thought. Just my luck, and Mom will walk through and ask who I'm calling. I dialed again.

It rang.

'Hello,' the sexy bass voice answered.

'Good evening, Sir,' I whispered. 'This is Jimmy, Sir, calling you as ordered, Sir.'

'Good boy,' the voice said. 'I'm pleased you called.'

I glowed. I'd done something right. I'd done something to please him.

'I liked your letter too boy.' I glowed even more.

'Yes Sir,' I breathed.

'You're very quiet boy, are you alone?' he asked.

'My folks are in the house,' I said, adding 'Sir' very quietly.

'I understand.'

'Thank you, Sir,' I whispered, relieved that I'd explained some of the domestic situation in my letter.

'Are you available on Friday boy?'

'Yes Sir,' I answered immediately, not caring if I had had anything planned, knowing that for this opportunity it would be sacrificed immediately.

'Good. You will be here at seven. Can you manage that?'

'Yes, Sir,' I said.

'Good. That is settled.'

'Thank you, Sir.'

'Do you have that jockstrap boy?'

'Yes, Sir.'

'When we have finished this call boy, you will go and put it on, is that clear?'

'Yes, Sir.'

'Does it have a pouch? For a cup?'

'It has a pouch, Sir, but I don't have a cup.'

'Pity. Can you buy one of those tomorrow?'

'Yes, Sir.'

'Good, then do that, boy, put the cup in as soon as you get it and keep it in until we meet. You do not take the jock off for anything, boy, is that clear?'

'Yes, Sir,' I answered trying to think about the practicalities.

'You will not touch your cock again until you are with me boy. You will piss through the jock and shower in it. You will wear it as it dries boy, and remember that you are doing it for me boy.'

'Yes, Sir,' I panted. My now untouchable cock had suddenly become rock hard.

'I will send you directions, boy,' he went on, 'in the post tomorrow.'

'Yes, Sir.'

'And I will see you at seven on Friday.'

'Yes, Sir.'

'Good night, boy, now go and put on that jock.' With those words, the phone went dead.

I took a deep breath and put the phone down. My cock was still rock hard. And I was not to touch it until Friday. I wanted to run to my room, but that would only attract unnecessary attention, so I tried to walk up the stairs as casually as I could. Even footsteps could provoke maternal enquiries. I was undoing my belt and unzipping my fly as I walked into my room.

My cock was still trying to burst out of my customary briefs as I pulled off my jeans. The jockstrap quickly came out of the drawer. Rather than rushing, my pace suddenly changed. I put the jock on the edge of my bed and knelt. Something ritualistic, almost metaphysical, was happening. I bent forward and kissed the pouch of the jock. Slowly, I stood and pulled down my briefs. My cock stood out erect. I picked up the jock and lifted it to my mouth. Again, I kissed the pouch.

Slowly as I pulled the jock into place, I realized what was happening. I was already placing my cock in the control of this Master.

Suddenly, I needed air.

I pulled on my jeans and boots and hurried downstairs.

'I'm going out,' I called as I pulled the front door behind me.

It was not a night to drive. The coolness of the denim in direct contact with my ass reminded me more of what I was doing as I walked towards the bar.

I grinned. I needed a beer. And I needed company to take my mind off the desire trying to burst out of the jock.

Anticipation

Sleep that night took forever to descend. I was unaccustomed to wearing a jockstrap in bed; I usually slept naked. The presence of the jock served only to increase my awareness of the decision. Eventually I dozed, my erection still pressing hard against the fabric.

I got up early as usual. It allowed me privacy and I could shower without rushing. I found it hard to believe what I was doing as I sat down to piss. It took a while, even when I remembered that I'd had a couple of beers the night before, but hadn't pissed before bed. I'd been too tired and too hard.

I lifted the shower head and sprayed it hard against the jock to take away the strong first piss of the day. It felt nice against my cock too – but there was nothing I could do about that. It seemed more than a little crazy trying to put my business suit on over a wet jockstrap. Then I came up with an idea. If there weren't worn briefs in the laundry at the end of the week, there'd be maternal questions. Folded, they helped absorb the moisture. It wouldn't be so bad after all.

With air flowing through the car, I felt almost dry by the time I reached work. Wearing a jock rather than briefs under a business suit felt strange, unusual. The Master had clearly intended the sensation to be so different that I would never be unaware of it.

My work suffered a little on the Monday as I'd been anticipating the evening's phone call. That Tuesday was the same. Rather than head for the staff restaurant, my lunch break saw me leaving the office and heading to the sports store across the park.

I hoped the Master was thinking about all of these emotions as I strode in. My heart was racing. I was too excited to be embarrassed as the store assistant asked what I wanted.

'A cup for a jock,' I answered, clearly and decisively.

It was only a few moments later that I was walking out with an awkwardly shaped package.

My return to the office was as fast as my departure. I was hot and I was in a hurry. I rushed into the building and headed for the men's room.

I dropped my pants and opened the package. I forced the cup protector passed my again throbbing cock and into the jockstrap pouch. I looked down. I was placing myself in restraint; constraint. Simply wanting to was amazing. Even though the Master was not physically there, he was present, and I didn't know his name or what he looked like. This, I thought, is progress.

That I'd suddenly found an apartment, and the freedom from my stepmother that I'd been seeking for so long was almost incidental.

* * *

I don't remember much if anything about that week – except the letter arriving on Wednesday.

It was brief. There was a map showing how to get to the Master's house and where I could park.

'Come to the door at 7pm exactly,' the letter said. 'You will be wearing a white tee-shirt, denim jeans and shining black boots. The door will be open. Come inside and lock it behind you. They key will be in the lock. There will be a sheet of instructions on a table to your right. Strip to your jockstrap before reading that paper.'

No hints. My excitement – and my cock – rose again. I'd spent that evening in my room cleaning my boots as they had never been cleaned before. Mom and Dad were – luckily – both out. It felt strangely right to be sitting there on the floor, wearing only a jockstrap, cleaning boots.

By Friday, I did know that the combined effect of the cup jock and abstinence had had their effect. It had been hard to keep my mind on the work tasks in hand. I kept looking at my watch, waiting for each minute to pass. Looking back, I feel sure my colleagues must have picked up on some tension. They'd have been crazy not to have done; I was in such a state. If any one of them had been looking carefully as I moved around, they'd have seen the strange ridge under my pants, below the waistband where the jockstrap fought to restrain the cup against my almost permanent erection.

I could hardly wait to leave that day. Yet, I knew I couldn't be out of the door at exactly four; that would have been far too obvious. I tried – I did try – to maintain some nonchalance, probably without any success whatsoever. I'd tidied my desk. I made myself take a trip to another office. I knew the person I said I was going to see was out, but it was yet another part of the charade, trying not to let my workmates see that I was so desperately impatient to be out of there. So, it was a few minutes after four when, as casually as I could act, I went and picked up my coat.

My departure at that time wasn't too unusual. I was always the first at the office. My normal commute was quicker if I drove the thirty miles before eight each morning. The others – who lived neared and used the bus or subway – customarily arrived nearer nine. The company had been one of the first to introduce flexible working; as long as the majority of the department were there between 10am and noon and two and four in the afternoon, we could choose for ourselves which hours we worked. The others were only too pleased to let me take the early shift.

'See you, have a good weekend,' I called as I picked up my bag.

Sheila, the head of department's PA, caught my eye.

'And, don't,' she said pointedly, 'do anything I wouldn't do.'

I wanted the earth to open. She had caught my vulnerable spot. I felt so embarrassed. For a moment, I was sure she knew exactly what was happening - the cup jock, the orders, the excitement, the lot.

I tried hard to look away. My face felt so red. I was sure it was glowing. I could see a little of Sheila reflected in a glass panel in a door. She was bending to put something in a purse.

'Especially,' she said, straightening up, 'don't drink too much.'

I smiled, relieved. Even so, I knew that the sooner I was away from her, from them all, the better.

The late afternoon was dry and sunny. People were coming out of all the offices nearby, trying to make as much of the nice day as the time after work allowed.

I was pleased to see that the parking lot was emptying quickly as I walked to the furthest corner. One advantage of arriving early was the choice of parking bays. Usually, lazily, I tried to get as near to the office as I could. That day, I'd deliberately chosen the most remote, darkest, and I hoped, the most secluded bay I could find.

I pulled my keys off my belt and opened the car door. I threw my bag onto the back seat and went to the trunk. There were two bags. One contained a white tee-shirt and a pair of jeans, the other a pair of black boots, spotlessly clean.

I took off the coat of my suit, being careful to take my notebook from the inside pocket, folded it carefully and laid it down. My tie came off next. I rolled it neatly and put it into one of the pockets.

Despite wanting to hurry, I knew there was plenty of time. I was not due to report until 7pm. The drive to the Master's house would only take an hour, ninety minutes at the very most even with heavy Friday evening traffic. I could afford to pace myself.

I put the boots in the passenger seat well and the jeans on the seat. The tee-shirt I rested over the seat back, taking care to make sure that it did not pick up any marks. I wanted the Master to see that I cared, that I was taking Him and the situation seriously, that this was not a joke, that He – and it – mattered.

I was sweating. I could feel it, as I opened the door and got in. I bent forward and untied the laces of my office shoes. I pulled them off and put them under the passenger seat. Next, I rolled the legs of the jeans and put them on top of the pedals. I looked round. Was anyone watching? Could anyone see?

Okay, I wasn't going to be naked in the car, but what would someone think of a jockstrap? A cup jock at that? And one that had been worn for four days and pissed through regularly? From looking around the local stores and the lack of imagination in their underwear departments, it was clear that anything other than plain white cotton boxer shorts or white BVDs would be either over-exciting or suspicious to anyone who happened to see me.

Yet, this additional nervousness didn't seem out of place. I suddenly realized why the Master had stressed that I should arrive at his house wearing something entirely different from my office suit. He knew that I would have to change somewhere – and that the very process of changing would include another frisson of excitement. He knew that if I'd changed using the men's room at the office, my cup jock was going to be more apparent under the tight faded jeans and that the 'look' – with the tight tee-shirt was also highly likely to be noticed and cause comment or provoke question. Similarly, he knew that if I chose a bar, there would be people who would see me going into a men's room the apparent epitome of corporate respectability and see me coming out looking like a Village People wannabe.

I took a deep breath and smiled. I didn't know this man. I had only spoken to him briefly, for two very short periods. Yet, I realized, I was getting to know him, how he thought and how he worked. Suddenly, I also realized that I was respecting that, admiring the technique and appreciating the imagination that meant that the interaction between us was already becoming far more intense. I had known that 'the scene' had started when I picked up the phone to call him. I hadn't grasped that he would be playing with me, with my mind, in other ways before I walked through his door. I then knew exactly why I'd knelt beside my bed and kissed the jock before I'd put it on. The ritual and the relationship had started at that moment.

I took more deep breaths. I wound down the car window. I looked round. There was a women two or three rows away getting into her car. The parking lot was even quieter now. The nearest vehicle was a pick-up, at least 50 yards away. I paused and wondered again what the Master would be like. I looked quickly around again, and then I undid the top button, unzipped the fly and pulled my pants quickly down. It was fiddly and awkward. I hit my head on the steering wheel several times as I tried to pull the dark blue wool pants over my ankles. The air felt cool around my butt and thighs. I was suddenly, dramatically, excitingly aware of the jock. Then, a tug and the pants were free. I sat back and dropped them on the seat beside me. Again, I looked around, still no one. I sighed, relieved. I bent down again. I don't know why, but I quickly realized that I'd have to put on one leg of the jeans at a time. I did the right first, then the left, finally pulling the waistband up nearly as far as my knees.

I looked up. Shit. There was someone coming towards me across the parking lot. I pressed my business shirt down as far as it would go. I was sure glad I'd decided to change that and put on the tee-shirt last of all. How do I look anything but suspicious, I wondered, bobbing up and down in a car parked in the furthest part of the lot? How would I explain my predicament? Again, my heart was racing. The man stopped. I relaxed, slightly. He looked round, then clearly seeing his own car, turned and strode towards it.

I leant back and raised my hips, bent and pulled the jeans up. It took some effort to get them over the cup. My cock had softened, but it was still tumescent, ready to react instantaneously to any further excitement or stimulation.

I got the top button done up, and a couple of buttons in the fly. I looked out of the car window. The lot wasn't as busy. I opened the door and got out. The man had driven away and once again the area was quiet. I reached inside for the tee-shirt. I rested it on the wheel while I undid my business shirt, took it off and dropped it, crumpled and sweaty, onto the seat. I didn't stop to think about the afternoon air hitting my naked torso; I reached for the tee-shirt and pulled it on as quickly as I could.

Yet again, I looked around; no one. I undid the jeans, pulled the jock into place, as comfortably as I could. I wanted to reach inside and adjust my cock and balls. I knew I shouldn't, but the temptation was great. Only the pressure of time and someone possibly coming stopped me. I pulled the straps of the jock tidy, tucked in the tee- shirt and buttoned up the jeans. I got back in again. It was awkward to put on the boots, especially without dirtying or scratching them. Yet, once on, I got out of the car again to lace them up. I folded the suit pants and the shirt. I went back to the trunk, put them neatly inside and remembered my black leather belt.

I caught my reflection in the side window as I went to get back in. I was certainly very different. The suit-wearing public relations professional had become a clone-like, a potential wannabe, leather slave boy. Tears welled up in the corners of my eyes.

Driving was hard. My mind didn't want to think about the road conditions. It was a struggle. I was glad that one of the tricks I'd been taught when learning to drive was to talk through everything I could see – from changes in the road surface, to signposts, traffic lights, pedestrians and the behaviors of other drivers. It wasn't a matter of potential madness, my father had explained, but safety – for me and for everyone else. Apart from which, he'd added, if you thought that you'd had a little too much to drink, it was probably the only way to keep your attention to driving as concentrated and focused as it needed to be.

Others, I noticed, as I waited in line for one set of lights to change, were singing along to the radio. I was talking through the road conditions – with occasional distractions, such as the chunky number in sweatpants at the bus stop and the jogger with wonderfully muscled thighs that I could see as I drove across a park. I had been right. The drive to the Master's house had only taken a little over an hour. The directions I had been given were certainly clear. I drove up the street slowly, looking intensely at the house. Was there any sign of life? The building was inconspicuous. It did not stand out from those around it. I don't know what I'd been expecting. It was a suburb. I knew gay men and kinky gay men lived in nice, comfortable, suburban homes. I knew there were playrooms and dungeons in such homes. It was almost as if I had been wanting to see a huge sign outside announcing the fact.

Instead, it was quiet.

I parked. I looked at my watch. In my nervousness, I was nearly an hour ahead of the time at which The Master had said I should report. My cock was hard in its plastic prison. My heart was again racing. It felt has if it had worked more that week than it did in a normal month. I could sit and wait in the car, perhaps drawing attention to myself from the neighbors or anyone else walking through the area, coming home late from a city office that Friday evening. There would be a continual temptation to touch my cock, to try to relieve the suspense, the tension.

What should I do? Trying not to stare too obviously at the Master's house, I got out of the car. At least by being in public, I would put the temptation to touch myself out of reach. As I walked passed the house, I felt certain I saw one of the curtains move, not a lot, but enough. I fought not to look directly. Then I remembered, there was a bar at the bottom of the hill – Dutch courage.

I stopped. Suddenly an excuse. I turned and went back to my car. In my bag in the trunk, I found the day's newspaper, I grabbed a pen and turned and walked away.

The bar was quiet. I was the only person there. The bartender was courteous and at first a little talkative. The conversation was small talk – the weather, sports, and 'my you're early aren't you? A bad day? Or wanting the weekend to start quickly?'

I hadn't had time to answer when he added: 'Well, if you'll excuse me, I have to fill some of these shelves before we get busy, I hope you don't mind.'

I didn't. I moved away from the counter and found a seat where I looked away from him, carefully positioning the newspaper so it covered the ridge of the cup jock in my jeans. I looked at the young man.

He was attractive, about six feet tall, with a nicely shaped chest and arms, and a strong jaw. As he turned round, I smiled; a paunch was beginning, probably the result of too many drinks accepted from other customers. The hang of his jeans and the way he reached to adjust himself every time he stood up suggested that if he was wearing any underwear at all, it was boxer shorts.

The fifty minutes went slowly, very slowly. The crossword was like a strange black-and-white grid pattern in front of my eyes. The words meant nothing. I tried to focus on the clues, but saw nothing apart from each minute of my freedom ticking slowly away.

The time seemed an eternity. The hands on the clock had never moved so slowly. A first beer had disappeared in seconds. I was dry but my hands were sweating. I must surely have appeared nervous, anxious, excited, but the bartender said nothing as he pulled me another. Did he see young men regularly, wearing jeans and white tee-shirts, coming into the bar between 6pm and seven, I wondered? His silence did nothing to make me change my mind. I certainly wasn't the first, I thought, and I'm very unlikely to be the last.

After twenty minutes of trying unsuccessfully to solve the crossword and keep my excitement under some degree of control, I had an idea.

'Do you have a phone I could use?' I asked next time the bartender looked my way.

'Sure, over there by the restrooms,' he said, pointing across the room.

'I walked across slowly, pulling a coin from my pocket. I took off my watch as I dialed the number.

It took me a couple of minutes and another two coins before I got my watch exactly on time with the speaking clock. If the Master wanted me at exactly seven o'clock, he was going to get me at exactly seven o'clock, I thought was I walked back to my beer and the newspaper.

At about quarter to the hour, I knew there was one other thing I had to do. I didn't think about some aspects until I'd started, such as being glad there was no one else in the men's room. Dutifully, I went into one of the cubicles, locked the door, dropped my jeans, sat down and pissed through the jock. I used tissues to absorb most of the moisture and put more over the jock, so the dampness wouldn't appear too obviously through my faded blue denim jeans. I'd learned such techniques the hard way during the week – and that the darker the pants for work, the less likely the dampness was to be apparent.

The second beer lasted longer. I made it last longer. Even so, as I left the men's room, I knew that I was leaving myself about eight minutes for a three-minute walk.

Was there an inkling of a smile on the edge of the bartender's lips as I waved and opened the door to leave? Now, all these years later, I still think there was.

I walked slowly back up the hill. I put the newspaper back in the trunk and checked the doors were locked. I took a deep breath and looked carefully at the house once more. I knew the Master had a live-in slave, but there was no sign of life whatsoever. There wasn't even a light visible through any of the windows. My nervousness increased.

I waited on the sidewalk and looked at my watch. Allowing 10 seconds to cross the yard, I took another deep breath and walked towards the house.

At the exact, ordered minute, I pushed on the door. It was open.

I went inside. I paused, caught my breath, tried to control my breathing, and then turned a locked the door behind me.

The room was elegant, simply but expensively furnished, unexpected and perhaps even out of place for an unsurprising house in an area not renowned for its affluence. The polished dining table looked, to my unskilled eye, like walnut. There were six elegant matching chairs. In the centre of the table, a decanter sat on a silver salver. The sideboard was also dark hardwood. It was not ornate. All there was on it was a bowl of apples. A large mirror took up most of one wall, adding light and size to the room. The impression was very unassuming but effective. A man of means, I thought, but not undue ostentation.

On the sizable dining table was a piece of paper. I walked across and picked it up. The instructions were neatly concise:

slave

1. Before reading this you were instructed to strip apart from your jockstrap. If you have not done so, do so now,

apart from the jockstrap before reading any further.

2. Leave *all* your personal possessions on the table. You may keep *nothing* with you. Whilst you are in your Master's care, everything necessary for your welfare will be provided.

3. You will find by the table a pair of black lace-up para boots and a pair of white socks. Put them on, making sure that the boots are tightly and neatly laced.

4. Ensure that your clothes are folded neatly and left in a pile on the floor by the fire.

5. If you wish to use the lavatory you should do so now. Remember always that you may neither remove the jock nor touch your cock. Leave the room tidy.

6. Your Master's Blackroom is on the top floor. As soon as you are ready, you will go up the stairs. Close the door firmly when you are in the Blackroom. Stand in the middle of the room at attention, but with your hands clasped together behind your back, in readiness for your new Master to inspect his property.

7. Remember – you are to remain silent unless asked a direct question. If this happens you are to commence each and every sentence with the words 'Sir, please Sir' and end every sentence with 'Sir, Thank you, Sir'.

8. You are now to proceed.

Meeting

I had made my first mistake.

I knew enough of the scene, its rituals and traditions to know that, for something like that, I could have been punished. Perhaps I should have been punished. I had not taken off my clothes before reading the instructions. I quickly looked round, feeling very guilty. There was no one to be seen, yet I still wondered if I was being watched.

I stood still and listened. I could hear nothing. The house

was silent, eerily silent. This man certainly knew how to play with emotions.

I was scared. I was excited. I could leave.

I could open the door. I could walk across the road. I could drive away. I could be polite and leave a note – scrawled on the instructions – apologizing.

I knew I could do none of those. I knew the decision had been made. It wasn't that I didn't have any choice. It wasn't that the situation wasn't consensual. The choice, the consent, had been made, been given, in the first phone call and the first letter.

I looked closely round that room. I studied it. I don't know what I was expecting to see, but despite trying to pay attention, I wish I could remember more about that room, that house.

I stopped. I took deep breaths. I stripped, but only as far as my jockstrap. It was still damp from my piss in the bar.

I looked at the instructions again. I was to leave all my possessions on the table. I emptied my pockets. My pocket book, car keys and small change were all that there was. My clothes were to be folded neatly. I picked them up from the floor and did as I had been ordered, far more neatly that if I had been in my own home. I placed my own boots neatly beside the pile of jeans, tee-shirt and socks.

I sat down. The floor was cold but clean. It was polished wood. The fireplace was spotless too, there was not a fleck of dust to be seen. A facetious thought flashed through my mind – you could still get the staff those days, but only with an appropriate remuneration package. I pulled the clean white socks and boots towards me. I pressed them to my nose. They smelled clean and fresh, but I couldn't help wondering who might have worn them before me. The boots were clean too. I wondered if my activities would be checked as soon as I went up the stairs.

It took a few minutes to lace the boots tightly and carefully. They felt good on my calves. I felt somehow strangely erotic wearing no more than the boots and the cup jock. I stood and took some more deep breaths. The time had come. I looked for the bathroom. I could see a light at the far end of the room. I walked quietly and carefully towards it; the heavy boots felt comfortable but somehow inappropriate on the elegantly polished floorboards. That, I thought, may be a punishment, kneeling and polishing the floor by hand.

My instinct had been correct. There was a small room, tiled entirely in white, with a toilet, small basin and a shower. A white hand towel had been set out on the edge of the basin. I sat and waited. It took a little time for my cock to respond. It had been almost fully erect. I had no idea how long it would be before I had the opportunity to piss again. With two large beers, I tried to maintain some sense of practicalities. It probably wasn't as long as I thought before the first drips appeared through the damp fabric of the jockstrap. I had again hoped for more indications of this man's way of life from the room, but there was nothing openly on show. The hand towel was made from Indian cotton and bore the brand name of a upscale department store, but it was not ostentatious.

I stood and looked at myself in the mirror. I was pleased with what I saw. I had not been good at exercise or sports at school, but I had made up for it in the last two years. The time at the gym was paying off. The pecs were developing nicely and my arms had a pleasant shape to them. I had a waist. There was still room, lots of room, for improvement. The front of the jock didn't look too yellow and working it with the shower each morning had prevented it from becoming too smelly.

I flushed the toilet.

Was I ready? It had been hard at times during the week

accepting that this was really what I wanted. It felt both demeaning, accepting such wishes from a man I had never met, but at the same time I had felt a huge pride welling up inside from simply being able to do it.

This wasn't like a bar pick-up. I couldn't offer coffee and walk away. Once the door in the attic space had closed behind me, I had – certainly for at least a few hours – abdicated my freedom.

Making decisions had never been a problem for me. Accepting them had. This was the point-of-no return in accepting this decision. I walked back through the dining room. I stopped quickly to check my clothes were tidy.

I walked slowly to the staircase. I took each step steadily determinedly. There were elegantly framed 19th century drawings spaced uniformly on the walls. Yes, the attire of jockstrap and boots did feel incongruous. If anyone else had been there I would have been embarrassed. Alone, trusted to enter this stranger's modest but affluent home, I felt uncomfortable. Was this, I wondered, yet another part of the mind trip?

When I got to the landing, I could see the ladder. As I made my way towards it, I looked round. All the doors were closed. There were no sounds. I looked closely. There were no indications of light from under any of the doors. The only illumination came from a light fitting on the wall.

I stopped at the bottom of the ladder. There was a trap door in the ceiling and a dim light. I tried to slow my breathing, with little success. I grasped the sides and took the first steps up towards the darkness. As my head became level with the opening I could see the structures in the shadows. I could make out a black painted wooden frame, some stocks and what looked like a massage table, but entirely in black. It took me a moment or two to become accustomed to the darkness. I turned and closed the trap door behind me and, trying to remember the instructions that I'd left downstairs behind me, wondered where to stand. It shouldn't be on the door, I thought. The Master would probably leave me for a few moments and then come up himself. Standing on the trapdoor and blocking his entry would not be a good idea. I moved a couple of steps forward and brought myself to the position the Master required, that unusual variant of attention and parade rest.

I closed my eyes and took deep breaths. The fantasy had ended when the trap door had closed. I had shut off my escape. This was reality.

Suddenly a noise in front of me interrupted my thoughts. I opened my eyes with a start.

Surprise

I hadn't expected the Master to be there already. I'd thought there would have been another entrance to the room. His instructions had been to enter the room, close the trapdoor behind me and wait. I'd expected to wait some time, to have an opportunity to think about my predicament, to think about the damp patch in my jock, my nakedness and what I was likely to find myself doing over the next few hours.

It wasn't to be.

I blinked, still trying to get used to the darkness as quickly as I could. There was a dark figure in front of me. I tried to concentrate. As instructed, I had left every personal possession downstairs, including my glasses. I tried to maintain a respectful downwards look, but examine as much of the figure as I could through my peripheral vision and poor focus. It wasn't easy.

As the figure became clearer, I could feel my cock fill and start to rise, pressing against the damp material of the tight jockstrap. He wore a black muir cap, the peak hiding much of his face. I could nevertheless see a strong jaw. He was clean-shaven and I couldn't see glasses. The mouth appeared firm and determined. He was wiry, a few tufts of gray hair peeked over the white tanktop he was wearing. A leather bar vest had just a single badge on it. He was wearing black leather gloves, tight black leather pants with a codpiece front and spotless boots that reached almost to his knees. He was nicely muscled, with good definition and very little body fat. He was in exceedingly good shape, I thought, for a man in his early forties.

I kept my head bowed as he walked slowly round me, first once then twice. He didn't touch me. He looked me up and down, almost clinically, his hands to his sides. I remembered the instructions. He would inspect his property. That was what he was doing.

It felt strange, being inspected in such an impersonal way, by this stranger, silent, and clad in black leather.

I tried to breathe deeply and slowly, to hold my stomach in, my chest out, nipples ready should he want to grasp them. I felt I could sense that he was appreciating my novice efforts. Although I may only have been twenty-two, I had made an effort to read as much as I could. In playing around and endangering other men before I had reached an age when it was legally permissible for me to have had sex with other males, I had started to learn. I hoped this man would teach me more. I couldn't see, but I could feel his breath on my back as he bent to look at my butt and upper thighs. A nervous frisson ran up my spine. I wanted to shiver in a mixture of excitement and anticipation; I fought the desire and tried to stand as still as I could.

I was still having to concentrate to direct my line of sight to the floor, a few feet in front of me, when he turned and walked away. He stopped just beyond my focal point. Very slowly, he turned. I could feel myself getting impatient. I wanted to know his reaction. Was I acceptable? Or would I be dismissed, there and then? I had tried so hard. I hoped he would appreciate my tentative efforts. I gritted my teeth.

I could feel my personal tension rising. I was sweating too. It wasn't because the room was too hot; it was comfortable, but not stifling. It was because of my nervousness. I felt the Master could sense it too, but I wasn't sure.

That he was standing, looking at me, without saying a word, made me think, hope, that my posture, predicament, submissiveness was giving him pleasure. I so, so, so wanted to do the right thing, behave appropriately, and bring him pleasure. I didn't know this man. I had spoken to him only briefly. Our communication had been very limited, yet I wanted to give him so much, to sublimate as much of myself as I could to provide him with pleasure and satisfaction by using my body and my mind. The black leather, the cap, the gloves all added to the eroticism, but it was his confidence, his portrayal of control that was causing a tightness in the pit of my stomach.

I closed my eyes again. I tensed my fists behind my back. I raised my head a little, then quickly realizing what I was doing returned rapidly to bowing. I opened my mouth slightly, swallowed hard and took some more long, slow, deep breaths.

He clearly noticed what I was doing. I was concentrating so hard that I didn't appreciate that he had moved towards me until a gloved hand touched each of my biceps. I gasped.

Again, I only just caught myself as my head started to go back.

'Good boy.'

He said just two words.

They were enough. I relaxed, relieved, pleased. Proud.

I had to control myself. I could feel tears welling up in the corners of my eyes, even at that moment, even so soon.

He held me as I fought to bring my breathing into a steady rhythm. I filled my chest.

'Sir, thank you Sir,' I responded. I hoped it was acceptable to speak at that point. I was trying desperately to remember the instructions that he had left for me on the table downstairs. I wished I had a better memory or had had more time to take them in. Suddenly, I remembered. I was to remain silent unless asked a direct question. I had already failed.

He didn't appear to react. Perhaps I was just fortunate, he was making allowances this early in the process. His reasons didn't matter to me then, I was just relieved, very relieved.

He let go of me and stepped back, but not for long. It was probably no more than a second, but felt like minutes before his gloved hands were back, caressing me, rubbing my skin. It was, as he had calculated perfectly, just what was necessary to help me relax. I could feel myself easing into his care.

My respect increased as I slowly became aware that he was reading me very carefully. None of the contact was intense, or violent. It was beautifully, disgustingly, sensuous. The intensity grew very slowly and gradually indeed, as he became confident that I was ready for it and indeed asking for it.

He grasped each buttock, gently at first, as if weighing each like a melon. It was only when I tentatively bent forward a little and opened my legs that his grip strengthened. From kneading the flesh, he dug his fingers in. Despite the leather of the gloves, I could feel the fingernails. I closed my eyes and my mouth became more tense as the grip became tighter. I offered prayers of thanks for the gloves. The sensations came in waves. Each slightly tighter and stronger than the last; he was reading me well. He would hold me a second or so into that beautiful juxtaposition of agony and ecstasy, where the sensation had become so intense that my mind couldn't decide whether I wanted to scream 'ooh' in pleasure or 'ow' in pain.

Suddenly his grip on my cheeks stopped. Again, I relaxed.

A gloved hand stroked my cheek.

I opened my eyes. He was looking directly at me, in to me.

'Good boy.' He said it again.

I bowed my head.

'Sir, thank you, Sir,' I whispered.

Again, the gloved hand stroked my cheek.

His attention shifted to my chest. Again, it was slow and gradual. Time was forgotten. A finger tip traced circles round each nipple, then a rosette of fingers would almost seek to draw out any tension from the pectoral muscles through each nipple, erect and sensitive. I closed my eyes to appreciate each delicious moment.

I knew the intensity would soon grow, yet the Master's skill was such that I didn't realize just how it was happening until the first 'ow' started to grow silently on my lips.

I opened my eyes. I could see a grin starting to form on his face. He took off the gloves. I tried to see the fingernails.

'Good boy,' he said again.

'Sir, thank you Sir,' I whispered. The emotion was different this time. I knew there was probably real pain to come. I wanted to take it, to enjoy and endure it, to give him pleasure. I hoped I could take the amount that would give him pleasure ....

The attention to my chest started again. I could feel the fingernails. I could see them now too. They had been carefully manicured. I could feel as they started to dig into the flesh, being drawn slowly, determinedly, towards each nipple.

It seemed a long time before he had each grasped firmly between the nails of the thumb and middle finger of each hand.

I opened my eyes again and looked directly into his. It was my first challenge.

'Yes. boy?' he asked slowly, just starting to increase the pressure.

'Sir, yes, Sir, thank you Sir,' I answered, taking as deep a breath as I could and closing my eyes.

Within seconds, the 'ow' had formed on my lips. I was so pleased he was working both nipples at once. My brain was almost overloading trying to decide whether one was being worked more strongly than the other and which hurt most.

My head went back. I could feel my face contorting, my lips tracing the shapes of 'oohs' and 'ows' as he slowly, then more quickly, then alternatively, then suddenly, dug his nails into my nipples.

I could feel the tears again welling up in the corners of my eyes. Then, in an instant, the nails were gone. There was just cool air. My eyebrows felt as if they were hitting my hairline. I glowed.

Trying to remain silent, I mouthed the words 'that was beautiful'. The slap across my face caught me by surprise.

It wasn't so hard that it really hurt, but the unexpectedness gave it power. My jaw dropped.

'Just don't take me for granted, boy', he said, smiling.

I sniggered.

'Sir, Yes Sir,' I answered. You are a sadist, I thought. This is going to be good.

* * *

That first night was really special. I have no idea how long he used and tested me. I remember being allowed, being directed down the ladder to the bathroom and being permitted to piss, but not before the damp cup jock had been put back in place. A toothbrush and toothpaste had been put out for me. I used them.

I could feel bruises starting to develop as I made my way back up the ladder. My Master was waiting right at the top for me. I kissed the toecaps of his boots as my mouth reached them. He bent and lifted me back into the room. It was then that he pointed at the cage in the roof space.

There, behind the bars, was a comforter and a stainless steel bowl. There was also a collar locked to the metal. The Master pointed. I entered, turned and knelt facing him. The collar was locked into place.

He had bent forward and patted my head before turning and climbing down the ladder. He closed the trap door behind him. I was alone, in the dark, locked in a cage with a collar around my neck, wearing a damp cup jock. The floor was hard, but it wasn't cold. I felt strangely good.

I had fallen asleep more quickly than I had expected. It wasn't until the trapdoor creaked with opening that I woke. I had no idea of the time. It could have been an hour later or eight hours later; I had no way of knowing.

I blinked. There was light coming up from the landing. It was daytime, I realized, trying hard to come to my senses quickly and ready to serve. I rubbed my eyes and pushed the comforter away from me as the form of the Master stepped through the trapdoor. He looked hot in a tight-fitting tee-shirt and jeans. I knelt with my face against the bars, my head bent as respectfully as I could. I watched as much as I could as the Master turned and closed the trapdoor behind him. He was wearing boots. He reached up and turned on a switch. There was more light than there had been when I had been locked in. It was whiter too, rather than the red light of the dungeon-like atmosphere before.

I couldn't bend far enough forward in the cage to kiss the boots as the Master stood against the bars. He pushed his groin forward. I bent forward and kissed the button-fly. A hand reached through the bars. It held my head close against him.

'Lick.'

Nothing more was said.

I put my hands behind my back and my tongue to work. As energetically as I could I ran my tongue up and down the denim, tracing and outline of a growing cock. I could feel my own cock starting to react and push against the cup jock. I had forgotten I was wearing it. I pushed my mouth forward and tried to chew. The material seemed very thick. Perhaps he was wearing underwear; I wondered what style. I could feel the balls against the fly. They weren't lying down towards one of his thighs. It wasn't boxers, I thought. As I chewed, I could feel the cock growing. It was lying up against his belly. Briefs, I thought. Nice.

My eyes were closed. My hands remained clasped behind my back. My tongue was out when he took half a step backwards.

'Stay there.'

I stayed. I kept my eyes closed, but I could hear a belt being undone. My mouth was still open when I felt the open button pressed against my tongue. 'Undo them.'

I went to work. It wasn't easy. The jeans were new. The metal studs took some effort to force back through the buttonholes, but slowly, steadily, one by one, I made progress. I was sorely tempted to open my eyes to see what underwear my Master had chosen.

'Keep those eyes closed, boy.'

It was almost as if he was reading my thoughts.

'Sir, yes, Sir,' I mumbled as I struggled with the last bottom button. When it was finally undone, he stepped back again. I could hear the denim being pushed over his butt.

'Now, boy', keeping your eyes closed, identify what I am wearing.'

'Sir, yes, Sir,' I answered. I drew in breath firmly.

'I want to know the style, the brand and the color, boy. Is that clear?'

'Sir, yes, Sir, that is clear, Sir.' My heart filled with dread.

'You said you liked underwear and knew the designs of different brands, boy, didn't you?'

'Yes, Sir, I did, Sir,' I answered, hoping I hadn't been too optimistic or too foolhardy.

'Then you'll get it right boy, won't you?'

'Yes Sir.'

'And you know what will happen if you don't?' 'I'll be punished, Sir?' I asked tremulously.

'That's right, boy. How I decide. Much as I might like punishing you, don't disappoint me, boy.'

'I'll try not to Sir,' I said.

I was wondering what he was wearing. The material had felt fairly thick. I could feel it as I was undoing the buttons. I hadn't taken that much notice. My attention had been on the task of the moment. I tried to remember. Cotton? I hoped so.

I knew Sir was American. What American brands did I know? Which could I remember? What were their differentiating features? Fruit of the Loom? BVDs? Hanes? I tried to remember. All had fairly similar fly fronts. All had narrow waistbands. All had standard brief sides. I could be having to guess. It was a one-in-three chance that I'd get it right; two in three that I'd be punished.

The Master was probably enjoying my discomfort.

'Are you ready, boy?'

'Sir, yes, Sir, I am, Sir.' I replied, ready for the impossible gamble. 'You have thirty seconds, boy, that's all.'

My heart sank. It really would be punishment.

'Did I tell you that?'

'No Sir, you didn't Sir.'

I was getting nervous. The Master could see that discomfort was close to becoming distress. He was enjoying my anxiety. I felt myself starting to sweat.

'The time starts ... now.'

He stepped forward. I bent forward and stuck out my tongue. I could feel the outline of his cock against the material. It wasn't fully erect, but it was filling by the second. I licked round the balls. The pouch ended. I tried the sides. The pouch ended there too. I could taste his pubic hair sticking out at the sides. I licked upwards. There was a wide waistband, far broader than most ordinary briefs. It was easier now, I thought, suddenly relieved. He was wearing a jockstrap.

I pulled back.

'Yes, boy?'

'It's a jock, Sir,' I said.

'Good boy,' he said, stroking my head, encouraging me, 'but that's not enough is it? The brand and the color?'

I grimaced.

'Shit,' I thought. I'd been in too much of a hurry in my relief. I bent forward again.

Would it be an American jock? No, the cock was pointing upwards and the material was double thickness. The texture felt like cotton; it was probably British.

'Litesome?' I asked, leaning back a little. 'Good boy.'

I sighed. I was two-thirds of the way there. I felt the edge of my mouth rise. I could appreciate the teasing. Did he have a colored Litesome? They weren't easy to find. He was an enthusiast, so he probably did. But, would he be wearing it? Would he expect me to know about the colors? I licked again. I went for the bottom of the waistband at the front. I put my teeth forward. Yes, there was a pouch. Hooray. And he was wearing the jock with the pouch on the outside. I was certainly fortunate. Litesome pouch jockstraps were only made in off white.

'It's white, Sir,' I said. 'How did you know, boy?'

'The pouch, Sir. They only make those in white, Sir.'

'Does it taste good?'

'Yes, Sir, it does, Sir.'

'Open your eyes.'

I obeyed. He looked good, so good. Wow, I thought, am I a lucky boy? I felt so happy, so horny, so right. He stepped back and took off his boots and then his jeans. I watched closely. His butt was tight. His thighs were nicely defined. I wanted to be there, taking off the boots for him.

As he turned, he caught me watching him.

'You like what you see?'

'Yes, Sir, I do Sir. You look good, Sir.'

'It takes work, boy.'

'Yes, Sir?'

'Are you prepared to work hard, boy?'

'Yes, Sir, I am, Sir.'

He reached towards a beam and lifted down a key. The padlock on the cage door was unlocked. He opened the door.

'Out, boy.'

I struggled through the narrow opening.

'And, kneel.'

'Yes, Sir.'

Obediently, I knelt on the floor in front of him.

Automatically, I bent my head and again closed my eyes. A

moment later, I felt the filled cotton pouch brush my nose.

'Lick.'

I went to work. I outlined the balls. I worked my tongue up and down the cock. It was erect inside the pouch. I kept my hands behind my back and my saliva glands as productive as I could. I had no idea how long I had been working before he spoke again.

'Pull it down, right down.'

I tried to grasp the waistband with my teeth. It took some effort, but I did it. I pulled it as far back as I could. This was the dangerous bit. One slip and the waistband would snap back against his cock ... and I'd really be in trouble.

It took a little time. The elastic was new. It was strong. Finally, I got it tucked under his balls. They were pushed up and out. The Master took the cue. He turned.

I took a risk. Before pulling the waistband at the back, I gently and courteously kissed each cheek of his firm muscular buttocks. It was very tempting to start licking them. I resisted and pulled the waistband down.

Once it was over the beautiful mounds, it was easier. He turned again and I pulled the pouch down between his thighs. He stepped back, reached for my chin and lifted my head. I took the hint and opened my eyes. He was looking directly at me.

'This is something for you to remember, boy. You never, never, touch or hold underwear your Master has worn with your hands unless you have special, express permission, boy. Is that clear?'

'Yes, Sir, that is clear Sir.'

'You use your mouth. Is that clear?'

'Yes, Sir, I use my mouth.'

'If I allow you in my room downstairs and there is underwear on the floor, you pick each item up with your mouth, one at a time. Is that clear too, boy?'

'Yes, Sir.'

'And, if I allow you to wash them, you carry them to the laundry in your mouth, one item at a time. Clear?'

'Yes, Sir, clear Sir.'

'If you are working with any other boys in my house, you each carry one item at a time, regardless of how many trips you have to make, or the rituals you go through each time.'

'Yes, Sir.'

'Good boy.'

He pushed my head down. His cock was still hard. It was large, full, circumcised and thickly veined.

'Suck.'

I did as I was told.

Peter's Discovery

'We've got plenty of time,' Peter said, as I made a start on my cereal. I was hungry. The hours of activity since my last meal had had an effect. I still didn't know what the time was. I didn't really want to know.

'The Master is a good man,' he said. 'He's gone out for a while, so I'm instructed to look after you until he gets back. He knows I'll take care of you.'

'Thanks,' I said, acknowledging his generosity. I looked at him curiously, wanting him to tell his story, from the beginning, as he had said.

Peter noticed. He smiled, his eyes directing me back to my food. I ate as quietly as I could, letting Peter tell his story in his own words.

I met the Master five years ago, he continued, letting me eat. I was an air steward, crossing the Atlantic, backwards and forwards, week after week. It was fun. I was young. I was, I thought then, fit, good-looking, cocky and confident, like many of us are, or were, in our twenties.

I was enjoying life. I would be in New York, then in London, or Paris, or Geneva. Those were the main routes I flew. New York was hot, very hot. I shared a small apartment in Brooklyn. I'd go in to the bars on the subway. If I needed to I'd come home in a cab. Otherwise, I'd stagger back on the subway again the following day. I knew what I wanted. I'd found that. But something was missing.

It was curious. Sometimes, I'd have been in the Mineshaft. A lot of the time, you never saw another guy's face. Sometimes you did. There were two, three, times when I'd be working and I'd come across a guy I'd seen there a few hours, or a few days before. I liked that.

One time, I'd had this guy on his knees. He'd been working for me. He was in his forties and in great shape. I had him using his tongue all over me, in the crevice of my ass, or washing my balls for most of the night. He was so respectful, so enthusiastic.

I had a collar. He wore it. I had a lead. I dragged him round with it, keeping him on his knees. I choked him, pulling it as he stumbled trying to keep up with me. I beat his shoulders with the end when he failed to keep his hands behind his back. I was so full of myself. I didn't know it at the time, but The Master was there. He saw what I was doing.

After letting this guy work for me all night, I walked away from him. I'd shot. I'd had a great time. I was hot, sweaty and tired, but I'd had my fix. The guy had helped me. It was beautiful, impersonal, immediate and the therapy that I'd needed.

I recognized the guy when he handed me his ticket as he walked on to the plane two nights later. His suit was clearly expensive. He was stylish, in a quiet way. You know how some guys spend money so that despite being expensive their clothes and accessories look cheap. He wasn't like that. It was restrained, careful, discrete. I admired him for that.

He recognized me too. There was a gleam in his eye.

'Good evening, Sir,' I said, stressing the 'Sir', making it very obvious, perhaps too obvious that I knew that for the next few hours our roles were reversed. He nodded courteously.

'Thank you, young man,' he replied.

'May I take your case, Sir?' I asked.

He handed me his briefcase and headed towards the first class cabin. I followed him attentively. I waited patiently behind him as he found his seat. I put his briefcase on the seat beside him. I knew it was free. I'd checked the seating earlier, to see how busy we'd be, but the businessman's name had meant nothing to me then. He was no more, no less, than yet another anonymous executive commuting between corporate commitments.

I left him for a few moments to bring the tray of champagne glasses.

He took one. He then opened the briefcase. I could see there was a small leather pouch in one corner.

'I trust this will be an interesting flight, young man?' he asked.

'I hope it is pleasant, Sir,' I replied, wondering what he had on his mind.

'Would you like it to be?' he asked, looking me pointedly.

It didn't take me more than an instant to answer him.

'Yes, Sir,' I said.

'Good. I think it could be pleasant and interesting for both of us.'

With that, he reached for the pouch and opened it. He handed me what I thought was a cockring. He smiled and looked towards the restroom. I knew that I shouldn't go while passengers were still boarding. I was taking more time than was really fair looking after a single traveler, but at least none of my colleagues in the cabin crew could accuse me of not being attentive to the airline's high-spending frequent flyers.

I rushed. I closed the door behind me and undid my zip fly and pulled down my jockstrap. I liked wearing a jock under my uniform suit. There was something 'unorthodox' about having a bare butt under the formality. The pouch held me more comfortably too. I'd tried letting everything swing in boxer shorts a few times, but it only took a careless colleague who forgot to put on the brake on a cart quickly enough to persuade me that I was safer nicely packaged. But, as I was saying, it wasn't until I snapped the leather strap into place that I realized that the strap was lined with sharp studs. I grimaced. I let the pouch back into place more carefully, zipped my pants and left as quickly as I could.

I walked determinedly back to my passenger. I wondered if I'd snapped the cockstrap on too tightly. When I was beside him, he looked up at me and smiled.

'Thank you, Sir,' I said.

As he said, it was an interesting flight. When I was serving him a drink, he dropped the napkin on the carpet beside him. As I bent to retrieve it, he stepped forcibly and firmly on my hand. From our roles in the Mineshaft, the places were truly reversed.

Although in my naive arrogance, I would never have admitted to anyone, I knew in myself that I was doing what I preferred to do. There was actually something exceedingly fulfilling about providing care and service for this imposing business-suited individual. In some ways, our earlier meeting didn't matter. I had found a different man. He may have looked the same physically, but to me, I was providing service in a way that I knew was a vital part of me. I also knew that the few intimate moments we enjoyed during that flight were just the surface of what could be so much more intense.

I returned the cockring to him as he left the plane. The exchange was over formal. One of my colleagues clearly noticed that the two of us had something going. He caught my eye and raised an eyebrow coyly. It was nothing, really. Most of us flirted with passengers. Sometimes we'd choose targets for one another. Sometimes we would gamble. It wasn't just the men. Everyone did it. We would get someone new to pay special attention to the grossest man on the flight. You know. Not the eldest, but someone middle-aged, usually overweight, over-arrogant and sweaty. The stereotype who we felt would be most likely to try and take advantage of the situation. It was cruel, but it was fun. My colleague that time thought my behavior nothing strange.

My meeting with the Master wasn't dissimilar. He came onto a flight to London too. He was smartly dressed and in first class. I hadn't noticed him until he spoke to me. I was serving him a drink when he looked directly into my eye and said 'You seemed to have a good time last night'.

I must admit I was shocked. I was confused. That time I was the one who'd been on his knees in the Mineshaft. I'd been wearing the collar. It hadn't been an especially good time, but it had served its purpose. Even though I had had the experience with the other guy, I didn't expect first class business passengers to have been in the Mineshaft. The Mineshaft was men in, or out of, leather. I wasn't accustomed to such directness either. I bowed my head as I responded quietly, and politely, 'Yes, Sir, I did, Sir'.

He didn't say much for the rest of the flight. I didn't know then what it was, but the Master had something about him. Now, I'd call it his self-assuredness. I know that his manner motivated me to make sure that I provided him with the best, most attentive but simultaneously the most discrete attention I could.

It was as we were getting ready to land that he spoke to me again. I was walking through the cabin collecting the last empty glasses and so on.

He beckoned and I responded.

'When are you working next?' he asked.

'The day after tomorrow, Sir,' I said.

It was an honest answer. I had a day's stopover before flying back to New York. I knew I'd have a bath and sleep most of that day and then I had decided that I would hit London's bars and perhaps a club that night. He handed me a business card.

'Seven thirty,' he said. 'Be smart. Be prompt.'

There was an address in Mayfair. I didn't have time to say anything before he waved me away.

He ignored my grin when he left the plane. Or at least I thought he did. I still think that he saw as much as he wanted to see, just enough to know that, yes, I would be there at 7.30 that night, I would be smart and I would be prompt.

My plans changed. In my bag were a pair of jeans, boots, a white tee-shirt and a denim jacket. I could wear my uniform pants, but I didn't want to appear at the address as an airline employee. I travelled to the hotel with the other crew members and had a bath. My cock was hard and my balls shriveled in the hot water. I wondered what was the best way to use my time. I knew that it would take me an hour at least to reach the West End from the airport. I knew too that it would take me a while to find some new clothes. I could try to get there and back or I could try and rest.

I decided rest was more important. I tried to sleep. I couldn't. I tried watching TV, but my mind was on this man in the dark pinstripe suit. I didn't want to smell of alcohol when I met him. I had one small Scotch. I had a second. The hardest decision was whether to wear underwear. All I had with me was the jockstrap I'd worn on the flight over and two others; one for that day and one for the next. I had a cockring too. I tossed a coin. Heads for a jock, tails nothing. It came down heads. I did the same to decide about the cockring. It was heads again.

Finally, at about three, I put on my denim and left. My hands were sweating as I rode the Underground from the airport towards central London. It felt a little strange wearing denim with my uniform socks and shoes, but it wasn't going to be for long. I was tempted to shop in Knightsbridge, but London was expensive. I could get clothes in New York far more cheaply. Apart from which, I didn't really need any new smart clothes.

I was fortunate. In one of the better chains of menswear stores on Oxford Street, I found a reasonable suit. I bought a plain white shirt, I knew that even a cheap white shirt could look presentable when it was new. The tie was my most extravagant purchase. It was silk. Whatever I did with the rest of the clothes, I knew that I would wear the tie again. I found a luggage store and bought a small hold-all.

It was nearly six by the time I walked from Oxford Street to find the address I had been given. I looked across from the other side of the square. I didn't want the man to see me, especially being so early and still in denim.

I walked round the corner and found a pub. I was lucky, it was quiet. There were only two other people in one of the bars. I bought myself a beer and retreated to the men's room. When I got back, my denim jeans had been replaced by the suit pants, a white shirt was over my tee-shirt. I'd kept on my denim jacket, so the transformation wasn't too obvious. I felt I should have something to eat, but my stomach was tense.

I folded the jeans and put them into the bag. I looked at the card. The man's name was Lucas Woods. I finished my beer. It was 6.45. I had three quarters of an hour and a walk that would probably take no more than four or five minutes. I wanted another beer. I didn't want another beer.

Although I had a ticket which would take me back to the airport that night, I had no idea how long I would be. One activity to pass the time became clear. I left the bar and walked towards the Bond Street Underground station. I checked the times of the last trains. I also checked the times of the first. It seemed sensible. I didn't know whether I'd be there five minutes or fifteen hours.

I walked along the street a short way. I took off my denim jacket and put it into the bag. I pulled on the suit jacket. It felt more as if I was going to work. By standing awkwardly, I managed to use the glass on a sign as a mirror. I tied the tie. It wasn't very well done, but it was enough for the time-being.

I walked to another bar. This time I had an orange juice. I didn't want alcohol and I didn't want a lot of liquid. I knew I could piss before I left there, but I didn't know when after that. I drank very slowly, very slowly indeed. My mind wandered. What was I doing there, in a strange bar? Waiting to see a man I didn't know? I'd already spent over $200 on what could be little more than a one night stand.

I'd never have paid more than a beer for sex in New York. I wasn't someone who needed to pay for sex, even when it was most convenient. The greatest expense I'd ever incurred, until now, was probably less than $100 – for a special meal for a special person on a special day - and the champagne, orange juice, eggs and flowers for breakfast the following morning. Was I crazy? I certainly wasn't that horny. Or was I?

It was 7.15 when I drained the glass. I picked up my bag and went to the men's room. I pissed. I washed my hands. I fixed my tie. This time it was knotted neatly. I brushed down the suit. It did look smart. How long the material would retain its look was another matter, but one that didn't concern me right now.

I walked back slowly towards the Square and the address I

had been given. I was still early. I walked around the Square. I noticed a cab draw up about fifty yards away. A couple came out of the elegant house. He was in an evening suit and black tie, she in a long dress. Formality was certainly part of their evening, I thought.

I timed my steps towards the door. He had said be prompt. I looked at the bell push labels. One said simply 'Lucas Woods'. I looked at my watch. It was 7.30pm. I pushed the button.

I heard nothing. I wondered if it was working. I put such thoughts from my mind. If it had failed, it would quickly have been repaired at such a prestige address, I thought. I waited for a buzz at the door or a disembodied voice from the entry phone apparatus. There was nothing.

I looked again at my watch. I pulled the card from my breast pocket and checked the number yet again. Although I knew the number, I was so nervous that I kept checking. I was looking for a sign at the end of the Square to make sure that I was at the right place. I was surprised when I heard the door opening behind me.

Mr Woods, the Master, was there, himself, in person. I must have been expecting a boy, a butler, staff, anyone but him. I tried to overcome my surprise as quickly as I could. He was wearing a business shirt, tie and suspenders, and half-glasses. He was carrying a whisky glass. He held the door open and beckoned for me to come in.

I obeyed and entered the tall hallway. I wanted to look around, but felt I should focus my attention. He opened a door to one side and indicated that I should go through. It was an office. There was a large, very large old-fashioned desk at one side, with a brass lamp in one corner. There was a large polished table at the other end of the room and between them two large leather settees. The decor was restrained. It was an impressive room.

Mr Woods went behind the desk and sat down. He motioned that I should stand at the other side. There were two chairs there, but it was clear that I should remain standing.

He looked me carefully up and down. I was being inspected. I felt embarrassed at the impersonality of it, it was almost clinical, but at the same I was pleased by the attention I was receiving. He slowly took of his glasses and put them down on a paper in front of him.

Peter's inspection

'I am pleased you are here,' he said, speaking at last.

I bowed my head a little, formally. Words didn't seem appropriate. I was already learning that the Master is a man of few words, at least spoken words, when actions will suffice.

'You seem to have made an effort, you were prompt and you are smart. That pleases me,' he said.

I glowed.

'Take off your clothes, slowly,' he commanded.

The room was a little above ground level. I supposed someone in a room across the Square may, just, have been able to see in, but if this man wasn't concerned about others' possible reactions, who was I to worry? I had a confidence in my body. Although I wasn't too well defined at that time, I wasn't carrying much body fat. All in all, as I've said, I felt good.

I took off my jacket. He indicated that I should put it on one of the chairs. I bent and untied my shoe laces and removed the shoes. I would try and make my strip as sensuous as I could, I thought. I then loosened my tie and removed it. I put it on the jacket, moving slowly and carefully. I undid my shirt, just letting it fall open a little. I turned to undo the trousers. The shirt had a long tail. I turned and took off my socks, laying them on the chair, and then the trousers. I folded them and put them down too. It was only then that I turned and faced him again. I looked at him straight on as I went to lift the shirt from my shoulders. I'm sure that he knew I had been teasing him and putting on a performance, but he didn't show it.

I took off the shirt and turned, folding it as I did, to put it down. I could feel the warm air on my butt. I hoped he liked the jockstrap. I didn't have to wait long to find out.

'Stop,' he said.

I turned and stood facing him again.

He looked at me closely again.

'Turn, bend over, and pull your ass cheeks apart,' he ordered.

I did so. It felt humiliating, but very erotic. I finally became aware that my cock was growing within the pouch of the jockstrap.

I could hear him moving behind me, but I remained still and quiet, I tried to calm myself by focusing on the carpet. It wasn't very successful. I could see his legs beside me. His plain black shoes were highly polished. I could see them as he walked right round me.

It was autumn, but it had been a hot summer in the US and I'd got a good tan on Fire Island on days when I hadn't been working. I'd worn my favorite tight Speedos and my ass was far paler than the rest of my skin. I don't have much body hair, although there is a little around my hole. What hair I have is a light color.

Even though I knew I was being inspected, the first touch came as something of a surprise. My body wanted to react and it took momentary effort to try and keep as still as I could. He ran his hand gently up the back of my thighs. He then cupped one of my buttocks and kneaded it, before suddenly grasping it hard and squeezed. It hurt very soon, but I held my position and controlled my breathing as carefully as I could before a hiss suddenly escaped through my teeth. A moment later he relaxed his grip. A finger grazed my hole. I thought he was going to enter me, but he waited for the muscle to respond then moved his hand on. I sensed him reach to the desk for a tissue; he wiped his finger. I thought for a moment that I might have had to lick it clean.

'Stand.'

It was another single word order.

I did as I was told. He was behind me. I felt his hands across my shoulders and down my sides. I hoped the shape of my back pleased him.

'Turn.'

I did.

Although I knew he was close, I wasn't prepared for the proximity. His face was almost in mine. I had a chance to look at him more closely for the first time. He had a strong jaw. There was a dark stubble fighting through, not surprising for the end of a day. The skin looked healthy. I was tempted to put out my tongue and lick it. I tried to focus straight ahead, on a point away from him. He saw what I was trying to do. When he saw that my line of sight was appropriate, he reached out to touch me again. He ran his hands around my neck, across my shoulders, down my sides. He picked up my hands and closely examined my fingers. I was glad the nails were neatly trimmed and clean.

He then reached for my nipples. They were reasonably well developed. I liked having them played with and chewed and having clips and weights on them, suction cups even. They were sensitive too. He grasped one and gently rolled it between his thumb and a finger. He did the same for the second. I closed my eyes and let my head fall back. His touch was beautifully sensuous. I wanted to throw my arms around him and fall to my knees. Having created the most delicious ecstasy, he quickly moved to replace it with a wonderful agony. He grasped each nipple between his nails. The pressure grew steadily. I could feel the pain starting to become more intense. Again, I didn't want him to see that I couldn't endure it, that I couldn't even enjoy it. I wanted to give him all of my most intimate sensations. I fought myself to take more. He could see my inner torment. If I had had my eyes open, I would have seen a smile begin to form on his lips. Instead, the intensity increased until the shape of my lips moved from being the ecstatic 'ah' to the agonized 'ow'. Another gasp escaped through my lips with a hiss.

'Open your eyes'.

Another pointed order. I obeyed. He looked closely into my eyes, my ears and finally prized open my mouth with his fingers. He looked at my teeth and ran his fingers round them, before running a single finger round between my teeth and gums. He then reached two fingers as far back into my mouth as he could.

It was hard not to choke, but I struggled. He was trying to check my reflexes and I think my endeavors pleased him. I hoped they would. It was only then that he finally reached down to my jockstrap. My cock had been hard for a while and was pushing up under the waistband. He cupped my balls and squeezed each, at first very gently, rolling each between his thumb and forefinger. Then, as he had with my nipples, the pressure grew, slowly, steadily, unrelentingly. Again, it wasn't until I let the sensations get to me that he finally backed off. He felt the outline of my cock in the jockstrap. He pulled the waistband forward and looked in at the bloated pink cockhead. It somehow didn't feel part of me. He reached in and pulled the skin as far forward over the cockhead as he could. I'm not cut and have a reasonable foreskin. It seemed to please him. He enjoyed letting the elastic snap back.

Again, I grimaced.

He grinned.

He returned to the other side of the desk and opened a drawer. I watched and reached in to remove some papers. He took a pen from the desktop. He handed them to me.

'Go and kneel on the mat and fill this in,' he said. 'The instructions are at the top of the first page. When you have finished it, put the pen and paper on the mat in front of you and place your hands behind your back. There is no need to hurry'.

I nodded, as courteously and respectfully as I could. I felt I should say something, but the words didn't come. I didn't know whether I should use his name, call him 'Mr Woods' or 'Sir'. Saying nothing solved that dilemma.

The papers were a questionnaire. It was the first time I had seen one, although nowadays they have become quite common. I answered as honestly as I could. Some questions had to be ticked if I liked the activity, several times if it was a real turn-on, crossed out if it was a 'no-no' or marked with a question mark if I was unsure. I filled in the section about my identity truthfully too. This man had trusted me with information about him and his activities. I could not do anything less. There were questions about whether I liked soldiers or sailors, leather or rubber, torture or 'dirty' scenes. It was difficult, because I felt so many such decisions would, and should, be taken by a master. 'I read and re-read carefully what I had written before signing the declaration at the bottom of the final sheet. I put the paper and pen down in front of me, bowed my head and put my hands behind my back.

I think he had been working, or reading, while I had been doing this. My attention was caught by a gentle double-knock on the door. I knew better than to look up, but I was curious.

Nothing had been said about me being seen in this predicament by anyone else. But, nothing had been said about anything.

I needn't have worried, even for a second.

'Come in,' he said and the door opened. I tried to see from the corners of my eyes, but had to lift my head. There, was a guy wearing tight Speedos, light blue, I remember them well, and boots, just like I am now. I looked as closely as I dared. His face was lined and he looked older, but he had the most amazing body. The thighs were muscular and defined, the butt looked pert, the abdomen was a six-pack that a teenager or twenty-yearold would have been proud of. His head was shaved. So too, as far as I could see, was his entire body. My cock jerked inside the jockstrap. Suddenly, I felt inadequate.

Mr Woods looked at the mat. This man followed his gaze and walked towards me. He bent and picked up the paper and pen before returning to the desk. He bowed formally before handing them forward.

There was a beauty and elegance to what was going on. The pace was so unhurried. The Mineshaft, the magazine stories, they portray a world where there is speed and violence. This was a gavotte rather than disco.

I gazed in awe at this man's body as the papers were read. I thought I could see the fading marks of bruises. The man's back looked as if it had been heavily beaten, possibly a week or so earlier. I was suddenly scared. What if he expected me to take a beating like that? I'd been flogged a few times, but never so hard that I'd been bruised. I'd seen men beaten with whips, the skin on their backs shredded, and known that such endurance was way beyond me. If he wanted to use me like that, I hoped he would introduce me gradually, gently, let me learn.

I closed my eyes and grinned a little. I was thinking

somehow I had been accepted, that I would be used. Yet, nothing had been said. Some people can create anxiety, tension and hatred with their looks and the way they move and stand. This man was exactly the opposite. He created calm, reassurance, acceptance. My cock was still hard. I was kneeling almost naked on a mat in an elegant London office in front of another almost naked man and Mr Woods, someone whom I had met during my work on and off during a six-hour transatlantic flight. Yet, I felt that calm. I felt that reassurance. I felt that acceptance. I felt very strangely, amazingly, as if I was in the right place. I felt fulfilled. And, nothing really had happened and nothing had been said.

Mr Woods looked at a tray of glass decanters on a table at one side of the room. The Speedo-clad stranger walked across and poured some amber liquid from one into a whisky tumbler. As he was doing this, Mr Woods got up from behind his desk and came to sit on one of the settees in front of me. He had brought the papers with him.

The whisky tumbler appeared on a silver salver beside him. He lifted it and took a sip.

The servant took a step back, bowed his head and held the tray carefully.

There was a silence while he savored the drink. I could smell the whisky. It was a while before he spoke.

'I am impressed, young man,' he said.

I felt honored and embarrassed. I looked up, like an eager young puppy waiting to please its master. I realized how ridiculous all this may seem to some people, and tried not to grin. I could not disguise my pleasure.

'I have a question for you,' he said.

'Yes, Sir,' I responded.

'Saying "Sir" felt right now.

I waited.

'Would you like to learn from Jan? You don't have to answer now,' he said.

My response was immediate.

'I will answer now, Sir, if I may?'

He nodded.

'I should like to learn, yes Sir, very much.'

He didn't stop me as I knelt forward and gently kissed each shoe.

The next words took me by surprise.

Mr Woods had turned towards Jan, I even knew this wonderful man's name now.

'Take him away,' he said.

Jan's actions were fast but light. He stepped forward, put a hand under my arm, helped me stand and directed me towards the door.

'I'll get the rest of your clothes later,' he whispered to me as he opened the door.

I didn't even have time to look back at Mr Woods.

Peter's recollection seemed familiar to me. Some of the way the Master behaved with him had been performed for me the previous evening. In some ways, I saw myself following in his footsteps, I could at least hope that I might have such a chance. I had finished my cereal a while before, but I hadn't wanted to interrupt Peter's flow. I put the bowl down as he took a sip of coffee.

'Shall I go on?', asked Peter.

'Please,' I answered. I felt I should be as polite and courteous with him as I should with the Master himself.

Entering service

Peter drank some more coffee before starting again.

I waited patiently for a few moments before he continued his story.

Jan took me along the corridor to what I can best describe as a servant's room or butler's pantry, said Peter. It was small, but cozy. There was a television set, a bean bag, and a thick rug in one corner. The other walls were like the galley on an airplane, counter tops and cupboards, crockery, and glassware, a sink and a dishwasher. There was a coffee machine and tea pots, a refrigerator, but no stove.

Jan pointed for me to sit on the rug.

'Coffee?' he asked.

'Decaf, if you have it, and I may,' I replied.

'Sure we do, but it will be instant. I am allowed the other, but it seems wrong to do it just for myself. I'm Jan, by the way,' he said, coming towards me and holding out his hand.

'And, I'm Peter,' I said.

That evening was interesting too.

Jan told me all about his own background, his training and his time with the Master. He was sixty, he said, and had been in service with the Master for ten years. Jan explained that The Master was extending his business interests in the United States and had bought a property there, not far from Washington, DC, which he would use as a home and a corporate base. He wanted Jan to oversee the setting up of the home. I could see why. Jan was not only physically beautiful, he had the skills of the best butler; household management certainly appeared to be a real strength.

'The Master is looking for someone, perhaps two people, who will assist me here in the UK,' Jan said, 'and two or three for the property in the States. He clearly thinks you have potential. What is your profession?'

He was pleased when I told him.

'Some of your skills may need refining,' he said, 'but you have the basics. That is good. You are working now?'

I nodded.

'How much time do you have available?'

I was in London nearly every week for a day or two, I told him, but I could transfer my base, by putting in a formal request. I didn't think the airline would have a problem with that, I said.

Jan nodded sagely.

'We shall have to see how you work out,' he said.

And that, Jimmy, said Peter, suddenly turning back to me, takes us to about where we are now. Jan is running the house in Maryland and he wants me to move back there. The Master is spending more time there too, which is why we moved here from the big house in London. He wants someone who can, in due course, move in here, look after the place and take care of him when he is in the UK. Just as the Master asked me if I would like to learn from Jan, I have been instructed to ask whether you would like to learn from me?

'I think you know the answer to that already,' I said, looking at the bronzed body. 'If I didn't, I wouldn't be sitting here now.'

Peter grinned.

'So,' I said, looking up at him, 'where do I start?'

'What has the Master told you?'

'You know about the listing?' I asked.

Peter nodded.

'I thought it was more sexual, but yes, the domesticity appeals. Please tell me more,' I said.

'Mr Woods is a strict man. He doesn't say a lot. He will praise you, in a few words, or pat your head if you have pleased him, or done something he likes. If you step out of line, you will be punished.

'And you will know about that too,' Peter added. 'He likes to beat people, and he likes his men to enjoy being beaten, so beating is a reward, never a punishment. Punishment is boredom and time-wasting. Take it from me, it is not pleasant.'

'In what way?' I asked.

'My experience of "punishment" had been the beatings of the Mineshaft,' responded Peter quietly, 'the situations where someone was told they were "a bad boy" because they had stopped licking their master's boots or had inadvertently touched their cock without permission. I was fascinated to find that there were others who considered beatings and floggings to be positive experiences, to be enjoyed rather than endured, creating wonderful neurological sensations rather than feelings of badness.'

He paused.

'You know Mr Woods is a physician?' he asked.

'No,' I had to say honestly, 'I didn't. I don't know anything really. Not about him. Or you. How did you meet? Please tell. It'll explain a lot.'

Courteously, he responded.

'As you'll have gathered, I'm a flight attendant. It was a few years ago, when Mr Woods was coming back here. When I was looking after him, during the flight, he said he'd seen me in the Mineshaft. He gave me his card when he was leaving the plane. He just said be prompt and be smart.

'When I said "Yes, Sir," I may have been obeying his instruction or just acknowledging the card. That was all he said though,' he said, grinning. 'And, look, I'm here now. You Jimmy are just the latest to find out that there sure is something about that guy.'

I smiled too.

'Just so you know Mr Woods' card doesn't even say that he's a physician,' explained Peter. 'He's not practising right now; he's advising two of the major pharmaceutical companies about the development and promotion of new products, that's why he is working both in the UK and in the United States. He also studied psychology. He doesn't like negativity. He wants his boys, his slaves, to grow and develop, to appreciate their humanity and to be valued and appreciated, perhaps, in time, even loved too. Does that make sense?'

'That makes great sense to me, Peter,' I said.

'He doesn't have time for those who feel the only way they can get attention is to "be bad" or mischievous. He likes those who have some self-confidence and self-esteem and don't need constant attention from him. He wants those who can appreciate that he values their presence, their appearance, their service even when he is at the other side of the Atlantic and who revel in the attention when they get it.'

'I understand,' I said. 'It sounds almost too good to be true.'

'There are some people who don't like him. They think that a slave is a slave is a slave, who should have no humanity, whose identity should only be a number, who should have no life outside a cell or a dungeon. Mr Woods isn't like that. However much he may own you – and he probably will – he recognizes that he can never assume your identity and, should anything happen to him, you must be able to survive. He wants us to depend on him, but not be entirely dependent on him. The difference is subtle. Not everyone appreciates it,' Peter explained.

'I may be young, but I think I do, Peter,' I said. 'Being too dependent scares me. I met a guy three years ago who was a total slave. He had no life of his own. Then, suddenly, his master was killed in a car accident. He collapsed psychologically. He just could not cope. If it hadn't been for one of his master's closest friends who had the space and facilities, he would probably have been homeless, may be even dead. He just could not manage the real world alone. It was tragic.'

'Yes,' Peter said. 'Mr Woods does not want to expose anyone of us to such a possibility. That is why arrangements are regularly reviewed to ensure that as much as possible is taken care of if anything did happen to him.'

'That's so reassuring,' I said. 'I sometimes lie in bed, thinking about this way of life. One friend tells me I intellectualize about it too much, but at this time, it seems difficult to reconcile the ideal of the slave, another human being, as "property", as a chattel, when so much attention is paid to universal human rights.'

'I appreciate what you are saying, Jimmy,' Peter responded, 'but I think that's a discussion for another time. We were talking about punishment.'

'Yes, I'm sorry. There is so much to think about,' I said, suddenly apologetic.

'Mr Woods likes us to look good. He will devise a diet for you and an exercise regime. You will have the diet prepared for you while you are here, or with him, or you will prepare it for yourself. He has his own very special and particular requirements too. You will learn the details in time,' Peter said.

'He has an almost schizophrenic attitude towards our cocks. We are not allowed to touch them. We must avoid touching them even when we piss. If you have a foreskin, touching is permitted for personal hygiene, but never anything more. Yet at the same time, he likes seeing them hard, or at least half-hard. That's why we all wear cock rings. He also likes the outline under tight Speedos or underwear. He also likes torturing cocks. You might have found that out already.'

I nodded.

'And balls too,' Peter continued. 'He likes to see what you have but also to know that it is out of the way. That's why we are rarely naked. He may tie your balls for you, but then they will be put away under a jockstrap. He may want your ass to be plugged, but you may still find you are then ordered to replace your Speedos.

'He also uses underwear to control and punish.'

I looked curious.

'I don't understand,' I said.

'He told you how to look after anything that he had worn?' Peter asked.

I nodded.

'Good, Peter said.

'None of us here has any items which are our own, I hope that's not a problem?' he asked.

'No,' I said. If anything, the idea appealed to me. I wanted to sniff and wear the Speedos Peter was wearing at that very moment. I remembered my schooldays. If I couldn't get near to the cock of a guy I fancied, I'd try to get close to something which had been close to it. I'd try and get to sniff and touch their swimwear or sportswear. I'd offer to take team kit back to the laundry, so I could take a detour to somewhere where I could jack off with my face in a jockstrap. It was the way I'd first got to try on a jock. It had felt wonderful, my cock and balls held tightly and warmly while there was still a cool breeze on my ass. I remember hoping the woman who ran the laundry wouldn't notice the damp patch on the pouch when I handed in the rolled up kit. I remember being at boarding school and going to one of the domestic staff saying I needed to get a clean handkerchief from the room where all our clothes were neatly stored, laid out on shelves, tidily named. I would rummage through the dirty laundry baskets to see if there was anything that had been worn by any of the guys who turned me on. If there wasn't I'd make do with something clean, kissing the pouch and wishing the gesture well on its route to a hot body and growing teenage cock. It was the guys who were on the way to becoming men who turned me on most. The bigger the cocks, heavier the balls and the hairier their thighs, the more I liked it.

'If he approves of you,' Peter said, suddenly regaining my attention, 'and you are invited back, as soon as you get home, you will provide a list of all the underwear you have. You will fax it here probably, then the Master will send you a list of what you are to wear and when. It will probably be a cup jock for two or three days before you visit though.'

'It was this time,' I said.

'Then when you come next time, you will bring everything with you, clean and worn. He will check to see what has been worn. Then, he will issue you with enough to last until your next visit. It may be what was your own; it may be something else. Sometimes, you may be allowed to wear something after he has worn it.'

'Oh, I'd like that,' I interrupting.

'Yes,' Peter agreed, 'there is something nice about that. But,' he paused briefly, 'to continue, there are other points. He may give you several items for one day, depending on your schedule. You will have to take those with you and telephone here to confirm that you have changed each time. He likes sending me out on errands, knowing that at a certain time I will have to look for a men's room to change and then a phone. He says it makes sure I focus on him. He's right. It does. And, having a choice made for you every day reminds you at the start of each day that he is there as a part of your life, even when you are not together.

'It is beautifully simple. It is not something so distracting that it could interfere with your work or your life, but it is enough for you never to forget his part in your existence.'

'Yes,' I said, 'it is clever.'

'It doesn't stop there,' Peter said. 'One principal duty either each day, or whenever Mr Woods decides, is to wash the underwear. It may be what you have worn or what he has worn or what each of us has worn. Every item is washed individually by hand. You can use the machine for spin drying and sometimes the tumble dryer, but Mr Woods doesn't like that.'

'That sounds straightforward enough,' I said.

'As I say, Jimmy, it doesn't stop there. If you are being punished, as soon as the items have been rinsed clean, Mr Woods will want to see them, in a bucket. If he is happy the water is clear, you will be ordered to go and drain the water from them and then go back to him. You will then be ordered to piss into the bucket. Sometimes, he may piss into the bucket. You will then have to wash everything all over again. You may have to do this only once. You may have to do it ten, fifteen, even twenty times. You have to remember to drink too, lots of water, so there you have piss ready if it's needed. You will never know which is the last one. It may take you an hour, it may take you all day.'

Peter looked at me, challenging me to respond. I took a deep breath.

'I get the idea,' I said. Yes, boredom and frustration could soon set in. It was a devious concept.

'You may find that being late with a phone call is enough,' Peter said, 'although if you are working, Mr Woods usually allows sufficient scope to avoid difficulties.'

'That is kind,' I said.

'Oh, yes, if you see something you like, do feel free to get it, but it will become part of the household. Bring it with you the next time you visit and offer it to the Master,' he said.

'I will.'

'He may also order you to go and buy something. If he does, you will be expected to do so usually that day, certainly the next. You will be expected to bring a dated receipt to prove that you did. You are not to open the packaging without express permission either,' Peter said.

'Is there anything else you want to know?' he asked.

Learning

It was a while before Mr Woods returned. Peter had shown me about the house. He had pointed out where toilet tissue was kept, where there were stacks of towels. We had even climbed to the attic play space and tidied up. Most of the work had been done in silence. Peter pointed and I obeyed.

When, once, I had started to ask a question, Peter had put his finger to his lips and whispered 'shush'.

Inside the front door, which I hadn't noticed when I had arrived the previous evening, was a small room. It contained two small closets, a shower and toilet. This, Peter explained, was our changing room. It was where we would leave our street clothes when we came into the house and put them on to go out. It was the only shower and toilet in the house we could use, unless specifically ordered otherwise. I had been honored that morning with using the Master's bathroom, Peter explained. Normally, we only went in there to clean it or to attend to the Master as he washed.

When we returned to the kitchen, Peter spoke again.

'This is the only room where we are permitted to speak,' Peter explained, 'perhaps I should have told you that.'

'I understand,' I said.

'The Master likes quiet. So, even when he is not in, I keep quiet. I am allowed music in my room, or the radio or TV, but not here. You will use my room when you are here, even if I'm not.'

'Thank you.'

'You won't need much. Everything is taken care of.' I nodded. That was already apparent.

I was standing, watching Peter as he started preparing a salad, when we heard the front door opening.

The sounds of two more doors opening and closing followed.

'Aren't you needed?' I asked.

'Not until I'm summoned. One of the reasons he bought this house was because it still had its Victorian bell system. There's a bell push in every room. We just had to move the box,' Peter said, pointing to an indicator panel beside the door. 'It didn't take long and it's exactly what he wants and needs.'

'Who goes?' I said.

'I do,' Peter said. 'If he wants anyone else, then I must go and fetch them. The responsibility falls on the senior boy or slave in the house at the time. Apart from the fact that I mustn't leave without permission, even to run to the local store for the newspaper in a morning, I have to make sure that I remember to tell anyone else in the house that I'm going too, so they know they are on call until I get back.'

'I do have some scope. If you're here,' he said, 'I could send you for the newspaper in the morning. I am supposed to report back that you, or anyone else, has behaved themselves and been appropriately obedient.'

I looked worried.

'Don't,' Peter said, noticing my expression, 'get too concerned, there is an honor among slaves. If you don't perform well, I would probably be punished too, for not supervising you properly or well enough. It's in my interest to make sure you know how to do your tasks well and efficiently, so I can report back that all is well.'

He smiled.

'How many of you, us, are there?' I said, pausing, wondering whether it was right for me to use the word 'us'.

'Here in the UK?' Peter said. 'Only two ... me and Morgan.'

I looked disappointed.

'But that may very soon become three,' Peter added, 'you never know.'

'I hope,' I said. Peter grinned. 'Who's Morgan?'

'You'll meet Morgan soon enough,' Peter said.

'That would be good,' I said, 'but, please, who is he? Won't you tell me something about him?'

Peter grinned.

'You're teasing me,' I said.

'And enjoying it,' he said.

'Ok,' I said, 'I'll wait. I'll ask him myself.'

'Morgan was the Master's personal trainer.'

'Interesting,' I said.

'Yes,' Peter said. 'It was. It is.'

We were interrupted. One of the bells was ringing. Peter looked up and reached for a towel to wipe his hands.

'Keep cutting the carrots,' he said to me, 'while I go and see what the Master wants.'

He handed me the towel as he turned and left the kitchen.

I hadn't done many vegetables when he returned a few moments later. I was trying to do them as neatly as Peter, but it was taking me far longer. I'd learn, I thought, I'll practise.

'He wants you,' Peter said firmly from the doorway. 'He's in his study.

'Which room's that?' I asked, trying to remember our earlier tour.

'Up the stairs and the third on the left,' Peter said. 'You know what to do?'

'I knock, go in when called, walk to the side of his desk and wait?'

'That's it, but make sure you have your hands behind your back, your legs slightly apart and your head bowed. Is that clear?'

'That's clear,' I said.

'Good. Go. Now. Quickly,' Peter said. 'He wants to talk to you.'

* * *

I went up the stairs as quickly and quietly as I could. One, two, three; I counted the doors. I stood back, took a deep breath and knocked.

'Come in.'

I opened the door, went in and turned to close it.

I walked across the elegant carpet towards the Master, sitting at his desk. There was a fire burning in the grate.

I stopped about four feet from the desk. I placed my hands behind my back and bowed my head. Looking down, the cup jock looked huge, and obscene; my stance was pushing it forward. I tried not to grin.

It was a few moments before the Master spoke. His broad chest filled a tight fitting white tee shirt. He had some papers on the desk in front of him. He took the half-glasses from his face before lifting his head to speak to me.

'Look at me, Jimmy,' he said. It was the first time he had used my name.

I raised my head to look directly into his eyes.

'You please me. Peter tells me you are already learning well and that you're not ... uncomfortable ... with some of the idiosyncrasies of our household here.' It sounded as if he was choosing his words carefully.

I nodded.

'You may speak, Jimmy, we are here to talk,' he said.

'Yes, Sir, thank you Sir,' I said.

'So? I said you were not uncomfortable with our arrangements. Is that correct?'

'Yes, Sir, that is correct. I like what Peter has told me Sir.'

I could feel my cock once again starting to respond affirmatively too, filling inside the cup jock.

'I am unorthodox, I am told,' he said. 'Others perceive me as a maverick. Does that bother you, Jimmy?'

'No, Sir,' I said.

Mr Woods looked at me.

'I think you want to add something to that Jimmy?'

'If I may, please Sir?'

'You may.'

'You seem a very sensible and caring Master, Sir. The arrangements Peter has told me about appear very good Sir. I don't see you as a maverick Sir.'

'You've had experience then Jimmy?' I blushed.

'Some, Sir,' I said, without wishing to go into detail.

'You know enough to enjoy stories about the Mineshaft. I saw that. How old are you? Remind me.'

'Twenty two, Sir.'

'Young,' he said, almost to himself, 'but not without potential.'

He paused.

'Tell me, when did you first experience feelings like this?'

I wasn't quite sure what he meant.

There were instances in my life that I knew had had definite effects on my personality. Perhaps I should start with those.

'There are several things, Sir,' I said.

He looked at me, nodding for me to continue.

'I remember my third birthday, Sir, just. I was told later that I had been ill and it was the first time I had been allowed out to play with my friends, Sir. I remember the door opening and the other children there for a party. One, a bigger boy, put me in a cart and started pushing me around, very quickly. Then, he put something, I can't remember what, over my head, so I couldn't see. It was exhilarating, Sir. I had to trust him, yet I could feel the motion. I was turned on, Sir.

'Then, a little later, Sir, I remember a game, again with other children where we were, in turns, tied to a chair. I remember getting excited by that Sir. There were other things too: the friend who had an old parachute harness; I loved being strapped into that Sir, especially when it was really tight between my legs. I remember going to the beach with one friend, Sir. He had an elder brother in his teens, Sir. I remember trying to spy round obstacles on the beach so that I could admire his body Sir. He also wore swim briefs that showed off a wonderful bulge Sir. I remember them to this day, Sir. They were gray. I remember even then I wanted to kiss his flat stomach and this bulge Sir. I wasn't interested in the boys of my own age, Sir. I wanted a man Sir. Other times when we went to the beach, I would leave the others and go exploring to see if I could see men with good bodies and tight swimwear, Sir.'

The Master nodded for me to continue.

'Then when I was at school, Sir, there was one boy, an older boy who I really fancied. He was seventeen then, I think Sir. He was in the gym team and really muscled. He wouldn't touch me Sir, but I could serve him Sir. He would make me stand at the corner of a desk, Sir, and then push my balls hard against the wood, with his foot against my butt, Sir. He started making me do forfeits. If I didn't do something he would spank me Sir. He would give me dares, Sir. Sometimes, if I did them, he would allow me to suck his cock, Sir, if I didn't he wouldn't Sir. He knew I liked being spanked, too, Sir. It took me a while to learn to like it Sir, but it was the only way I could get him to touch my bare skin, Sir, so I did it Sir, and got to enjoy it too Sir.

'He quickly got to know that I'd do a lot to get access to his body and cock Sir. We wore rough wool trousers Sir. Sometimes, he would tell me to go to the rest room and take off my underwear Sir and take it to him. Then he'd tell me to meet him somewhere an hour or so later. I would be itching and scratching so much by then, Sir.

'He would make me undo his trousers with my mouth and teeth Sir. He wouldn't let me touch him with my hands at all sometimes, Sir. He was the first guy to use my ass Sir and get me to lick ass too Sir.

'I can't remember how or why, but we'd got into a lockable store Sir. He asked me if I wanted it. I said yes, thinking it would be there to suck. He told me to stand and drop my trousers Sir and turn round. I did, not knowing what he would do. The next thing I knew something greasy was being smeared on my asshole Sir and I could feel him trying to enter me Sir. It wasn't that good, Sir. He got into me, just, a little way, and then in a few thrusts, it was all over, Sir. I was trying to pull my shirt up my back so I could feel more of his body against me, Sir. I hadn't known about fucking until then, Sir.

'He started calling me "queer" and "faggot" after that Sir. He said he hadn't enjoyed it and didn't like himself for doing it, but he kept on using me Sir. Another time, he was lying on the floor. He pulled his legs up and let me lick his ballsac Sir. I had to keep my hands behind my back. I don't think I was allowed to undress at all Sir. Then, suddenly, he pushed my head down so I was licking his ass. I was shocked, perhaps disgusted, but he tasted good and his ass started to open. It wasn't until later that I wondered how much it had been used, Sir. Once I'd started work there, Sir, he hardly had to touch himself before he shot, Sir. He taught me to hold my hand in front of his cock so I could catch his cum, Sir, and then lick it up, Sir. When he had gone, Sir, I would jerk off, sometimes two or three times, Sir.

'When he called me names, Sir, I didn't deny any of them, Sir, I couldn't. I knew. He introduced me to chewing on a jockstrap Sir. He'd say I had to work to earn his cock or balls, Sir. Those are some of the things that got me started Sir,' I said.

'A good and thorough introduction, Jimmy,' he said.

'Thank you Sir. Sir?' I asked.

'Yes, Jimmy,' the Master said.

'Sir, you know how some people seem to think it is always adults who prey on young men?'

'I do, Jimmy.'

'For me it was the other way round, Sir. I was trying to get to the men Sir. Thinking back, Sir, I put some people in quite serious danger.'

'I understand, Jimmy. I understand.'

It was a moment or two before he spoke again.

'This part of your life is important to you, obviously.'

'Yes, Sir, I said.

'How important?'

'Very, Sir.'

'Would you make sacrifices?'

'Such as, Sir?'

'Making it your entire non-working life?'

The question caught me by surprise.

The Master looked at me.

'Yes, Sir. I would.' The answer came so quickly that I was surprised with myself.

The Master stood. He picked up the papers from the desk and came round to me.

'There is some more information about you I need,' he said.

'Fill in this form. You may kneel over there, on the mat in front of the fire.'

He handed me a pen too. I did as I was told.

As I knelt, the Master pressed a button at the side of the desk. It took a couple of minutes before there was a knock at the door.

Peter came in when called.

'Is Morgan clean?' the Master asked.

'Yes, Sir,' said Peter.

'Good. Plug him at six, put him in a straitjacket at seven, a head harness at 7.30 and have him kneeling ready upstairs at eight. I shall eat at 6.30. Is that clear?'

'Yes, Sir,' Peter said.

It was hard to keep my attention on the questionnaire in front of me. Mention of Morgan had me wondering. Peter had told me a little, but I wanted to know more. I was curious. What would the Master do to him once he was upstairs? For a moment, I wished that I would not be leaving later and that I could stay around and find out. It was a moment or two later before I realized that even if I did stay, there was no reason I would be allowed to witness what happened or even find out about it. Another irony of my predicament hit me: At one moment I had no privacy, yet seconds later no one else could know what was happening, what was being done to me. I tried not to think about. It was too much for my head to cope with. It was hard to focus on the paper. There were lots of questions. They were probably the same questions that Peter had answered. I wanted to respond as honestly as I could.

'Don't worry about filling in details of your measurements or sizes,' Mr Woods said suddenly. 'Peter will measure you later. There were some in your letter, weren't there?'

'Yes, Sir, there were,' I said.

On trial

I wasn't sure what to do when I'd finished. I read the questions again, and my answers. The instructions had said that all the answers should be full sentences. It had been tempting to respond with one-word answers, but I had concentrated and tried to do everything correctly. I had tried to avoid spelling mistakes too. Towards the end, space had been left for me to describe fantasies and experiences. I hoped that one I day I may be able to have copies of these. I had tried to describe well a dream and something that had really happened to me, only a few days earlier.

Should I interrupt Mr Woods and tell him that I had finished? Or should I wait for him to notice? I decided that it was probably more important not to disturb him. I carefully laid the papers and pen down on the mat in front of me and sat back on my haunches. I was glad I was wearing the cup jock. My cock had been really hard as I described the fantasy and the experience. I felt that I would have been embarrassed if I had been naked with so strong an erection, but again, ironically, I knew that embarrassment may well no longer have any place in my life.

It took a while for Mr Woods to notice. He was engrossed in the work on his desk. I must admit that I didn't mind. It had given me time to look more closely at him and the room. There were shelves full of books. Some, larger volumes, were closer to the floor, coffee-table tomes of art and history. I could see rows of hardback texts, probably academic, but I couldn't read the titles from where I was sitting. There was a shelf full of LPs, but again I couldn't identify any particular music.

All the wood that was visible, in the furniture and shelves, was dark. The door and window frames were white. The drapes were heavy, dark maroon and reached the floor. The decor was simple with more prints and certificates on one wall. There was a huge mirror over the fireplace and opposite it a modern painting. I thought it was probably a Hockney. It was huge, nearly six feet square. I couldn't remember

Hockney having painted anything so large. Even so, it was an impressive piece of work and an impressive statement of affluence. I was considering it closely when Mr Woods looked up. He gestured for me to pick up the papers and return them to his desk. I wondered how such a small motion could indicate so much as I stood. I lowered my head as I stood in front of him and handed him the sheets.

'You realize there has been a change?'

I looked surprised.

'I don't understand, Sir,' I said.

'Do you remember my original listing, boy? The one you answered?'

'A little Sir,' I said, hesitating and trying to rack my memory.

'Do you remember what it said?'

'That you had a blackroom, Sir?' I said, still trying to remember. 'Your age, and that you would provide training, Sir?'

'That's true, boy,' Mr Woods said, 'but that was all.'

That I was puzzled and confused must have shown.

'It said nothing about permanence or servitude, boy. That's what has changed.'

I felt relieved that I hadn't missed something more significant. I still wasn't quite sure what Mr Woods was saying. Training, to me at least, had connotations of a continuing commitment. I had read the original listing as meaning something more than a one-night stand or a single scene.

'Yes, Sir,' I said, as noncommittally as I could.

'Look at me.' The command was quiet but firm.

'You still haven't realized what I am saying, have you boy?'

'No, Sir,' I admitted, hoping again that I hadn't failed him so soon.

'That listing was about play, boy, about blackroom training.'

'Yes, Sir,' I said.

'I will be blunt. You have seen some of how my household functions. You have met Peter. He has told you what goes on?'

'A fair amount, yes, Sir,' I said.

'Good. Did he tell you I need another boy?'

It suddenly made sense. Peter had mentioned the Master's requirements. I thought that so soon, with so little time, it would have been too soon for him to have considered me seriously. I hadn't paid enough attention to Peter's earlier comments.

'Yes, Sir, he did, Sir,' I said. I could feel a smile starting to appear on my face.

'And, boy?' Mr Woods face was lightening now too.

'Sir ....' I didn't know what else to say. The feeling was joyous. I was close to tears. I could feel them welling up in the corners of my eyes. Was I really this close to someone as skilled and good-looking as Mr Woods? With a household that included someone like Peter? I could hardly believe my good fortune.

Mr Woods let himself grin. He looked at me coyly, over the top of his glasses.

I wanted to fall to my knees and kiss his feet. He knew that. He enjoyed keeping me standing there, hands behind my back, dressed only in my cup jock.

'It is not permanent, boy, yet.'

I wasn't sure whether to be glad or sad. I had something. It was there. I had no idea how long it would last. That was probably in my hands, but I had a chance. I was delighted, and daunted at the same time.

'Yes, Sir,' I said.

'Has Peter told you of our requirements?'

'Some of them, Sir, yes,' I said.

'And?'

'They seem highly appropriate, Sir,' I said. I wanted to say I thought they were good and a turn-on, but it seemed better to moderate my language. Should slaves praise Masters? Commend, perhaps, praise, I thought, seemed a little too much.

'You will provide Peter with the information he asked you for, as quickly as you can, is that clear?'

'Yes, Sir, that is clear.'

'I shall want, through him, to know when you are available. I shall expect you to maintain your commitments,' he said, looking at me directly. I knew he had high expectations.

'I understand, Sir,' I said.

'Good, I need to know that,' he said. 'It does not mean that I am not understanding and compassionate. What work do you do?'

'I'm an assistant Sir, a researcher, just starting out, Sir, more like a PA than anything else, Sir,' I said.

Mr Woods smiled. 'That's good. Your hours?'

'Usually nine to five, eight until four, Sir, unless there's something special happening or an emergency.'

'What line of business?'

'Public relations, Sir.'

'Are there many emergencies?'

'Perhaps once every two weeks or so, Sir, and we're on-call to journalists out-of-hours, on a rota.' I answered trying to think about my weekend duties and responsibilities. 'The company has some emergency response clients, Sir, so it depends what happens to them.'

'And when something happens, there's not a lot you can do about changing your work hours, is there?'

'Not a lot, no Sir,' I said. 'Not if I'm there when it happens.'

'I understand,' he said. 'Family?'

'I've been living with my Mom and Dad, Sir, or rather my stepmother, Sir. I'm an only child.'

'That's good,' he said. 'And your living arrangements?'

'I'm sharing an apartment, Sir. I moved in a few days ago.'

'Who with? A male or female?'

'A male, Sir, a former colleague,' I said.

'Does he know?'

'A little, Sir,' I said, 'that I'm gay. He is too Sir, but ....'

'Yes, boy?'

'He's not as... well, Sir... he's more... vanilla, Sir,' I said, unsure about my terminology.

'I understand that too, boy. He needn't know anything, perhaps except the fact that you may be away more evenings or weekends, need he?'

'No, Sir.'

'If he was to ask?'

'I'd tell him, Sir,' I said, 'as much as I thought he needed to know.'

'I see,' he said.

Mr Woods looked at me thoughtfully.

He paused for a while.

'What if I was to require that you only wore Speedos, and perhaps a tee-shirt, at home, boy? What would he say to that?' he asked.

'Well, Sir, I often wear shorts,' I said, honestly.

'What sort?'

'Usually tight, Sir, or cycling shorts sometimes after the gym, Sir,' I said. 'Whenever I can Sir.'

I thought about the extra freedoms of the apartment, compared with my parents' home. Dad would probably have liked having the heating up enough to wander around wearing shorts, probably even less. Mom was too concerned about modesty and heating bills.

'You didn't answer my question, boy.' The Master pulled back my attention.

I blushed.

'I'm sorry, Sir.'

'How would your roommate react to Speedos? Now, honestly, boy,' he said, 'tell me.'

I tried to think what Brian's reactions might be; I had no way of knowing. I thought I had better be cautious.

'He'd be curious Sir,' I said. 'He might think it a bit much, especially if he had friends coming round.'

'That's better, boy,' he said. 'I had expected something like that. It's not unreasonable.'

I felt relieved.

Mr Woods then opened one of the desk drawers. He pulled out some money. He pushed some cash towards me.

'Tomorrow, you will buy two pairs of square-cut Speedos. You know the style, I mean?'

'Yes, Sir, I do, Sir,' I said.

'Make sure they are reasonably tight. They can be a dark color, if you wish, but you will wear them with a cock ring, when your roommate is at home. Is that clear?'

'Yes, Sir.'

'You will mail me the receipt. I expect to see tomorrow's date on it. If they cost any more than this,' he said, looking down at the note, 'I will reimburse you when we next meet. Do you have some standard, brief-style Speedos?'

'Yes, Sir.'

'You will wear those whenever he is out.' 'Yes Sir.'

'If you wish, you may one pair under the others, so you can take them off and put them on as he goes in and out, if that is likely to happen. Is that clear?'

'Yes, Sir,' I said, nodding.

'You know about my instructions?'

'Peter told me, yes Sir.'

'I will issue those as soon as I get your list. You will change into the Speedos as soon as you get home each day. You will sleep in a cup jock. When do you shower?'

'Usually in the morning, Sir,' I said.

'Good, that's when I like my boys to get clean. You may only touch your cock to wash it.'

'Yes, Sir.'

'Good. Your Master is only interested in occasional slaves for use in the blackroom. You appear ready for something more permanent involving servitude. You also seem to know and accept that you must be prepared to many an on-going and regular commitment to your Master. You will be required to come here regularly, but then you know that now, don't you, boy?'

'Yes, Sir, I do, Sir.' I said.

'Let me see.' Mr Woods looked to a book on his desk. It was his calendar. 'When are you likely to be available next boy?'

'Any evening, Sir, but I need to be in work for eight each morning, Sir.'

Mr Woods looked up at me. 'I understand, boy, and admire your enthusiasm. However, I think that for the time-being that may be a little unrealistic, don't you? The commute is, what, nearly an hour? By the time you have had something to eat and if you need to be out of here early in the morning to get back, it won't allow much time. We shall may be have to think about that in the future. The weekend then boy?'

'Yes, Sir. Friday, Sir?' I asked, hopefully.

'I don't see why not. You made it here without any problems last night, didn't you?'

'Yes, Sir.'

'You were even early.'

I blushed. I had hoped that he hadn't noticed. I wondered how he had, or whether Peter had told him.

'Yes, Sir, I was.'

'That needn't be a problem any more. I shall tell Peter to expect you at six. You can use the room downstairs. He will have something for you to eat. I will instruct you further during the week.'

'Yes, Sir.'

'What are you to do for me, boy? Repeat my instructions, then I know you will have remembered them clearly.'

'I am to buy two square-cut Speedos tomorrow, Sir and mail you the receipt. I am to wear them whenever my roommate is in the apartment, Sir, and ordinary Speedos when he is not Sir, and a cup jock at nights. Oh, yes, Sir,' I said remembering, 'and a cockring too, Sir.'

'And, boy?'

'I'm not to touch myself, Sir,' I said, still a little bashfully, 'except to wash in the mornings, Sir.'

'You will not wash the Speedos; you will wear the new ones on alternate days and you will bring them all with you on Friday. Can you wear a cup jock to work, boy?'

'I did for two days this week, Sir,' I said. I had been awkwardly aware of a strange bulge in my pants, but no one in the office seemed to have noticed. If they had, they hadn't said anything. I'd been more careful than usual at home about wearing a robe or carrying a towel when going to the bathroom. I hadn't wanted to answer any curious questions from Brian then.

'Then you will do so again. You will wear that one,' he said, looking down to my groin, 'and you can wear it each night.'

'Yes, Sir,' I said, wondering just how much extra deodorant I might need by the time Friday had arrived.

Mr Woods sat quietly. It was a few moments before he spoke again.

'I think that's all for the time being. I think you know that you have impressed me, boy. I shall be looking forward to

Friday,' he smiled, looking up at me as he spoke. 'Dismissed.'

I was at a loss. I'd just encountered another irony: the commands from the seated Master to the standing slave. I wasn't quite ready to be discharged so suddenly. I wondered what I should do. I wondered if I should say anything.

Mr Woods' gaze had returned to the papers on his desk. He was starting to read what I had written. A spoken response seemed wrong. I bowed, a little stiffly, but that seemed right. I walked to the door as lightly as I could and opened and closed it as quietly as possible. Outside, I paused for a moment.

'Wow,' I thought. There was no other expression for it.

Morgan's surprise

Peter was waiting for me in the kitchen.

'So?' he said.

'I'm on trial,' I said. 'I think that's the best way to describe it.'

'Not what you were expecting?'

'Well, certainly not this time yesterday,' I said.

Peter handed me a mug. I drank the coffee quickly. I hadn't noticed the thirst. Nerves, excitement, I thought. It was only when I put the mug down that I noticed Morgan.

He was sitting across the room on the bean bag, where Peter and I had spoken earlier.

'Hi,' I said, walking towards him. I felt a little more confident now that I was at least temporarily a member of the household. I held out my hand.

'I'm not sure how formal I should be,' I said. 'Peter told me it was okay to talk and be friendly in here.'

Morgan smiled and started to get up, holding out his hand to meet mine. It was only as he started to straighten that I noticed the metal band round his waist and the metal plate at his front.

'Wow!' I stopped suddenly, just as I'd grasped Morgan's hand.

He grinned.

'Yeh,' he said, 'I like it too.'

I was stunned. I'd heard of chastity belts for slaves, but never seen one before. My mouth was still hanging open in surprise. Peter had come up behind me.

'If you're lucky, you might get one too one day,' Peter said to me, tapping the cup of my jock. 'They're certainly more effective than any piece of molded plastic.'

I wasn't interested in my own predicament right at that moment. It was Morgan who was fascinating me. There was a narrow metal band round his waist. It looked as if it had some sort of rubber around it to stop the edges cutting into his flesh. A plate, about four or five inches wide where it met the waistband, ran down between his legs, tapering as it did. Each of his balls was pushed out to the side of the metal plate. I could see two cylinder locks, one on the waistband and another halfway down the plate. Morgan was following my inspection. He turned so I could see two chains running from between his legs to the back of a waistband, like the straps of a jock. 'The cock is in a tube pointing downwards,' he said, answering my question before I had had a chance to even think about asking it.

'And the Master has the key,' he added, smiling.

I could feel my own cock hardening yet again. I was still amazed.

'It's been on for three weeks now,' Morgan said.

'Three weeks?' I could hardly keep the incredulity from my voice.

'Let me explain,' he said. 'I'm always being asked.'

'I'm sure you are,' I said, striving not to sound too facetious.

'It was made to measure. I can do anything in it, even go to the gym. Okay, I have to sit down to piss, and I can get a little hard, I can just,' he said bending and reaching down back between his legs, 'just touch the cock head. Look.'

Morgan turned and bent forward. I could just see the bottom of the head of his cock poking out of a metal tube. It looked as if there was a ring running through a hole in the tube.

'And, yes, I do have a Prince Albert piercing that's locked to the tube too,' he said, again before I had had time to ask.

'Don't you get frustrated?' I asked, hoping my enquiry didn't sound too naive.

'Sure I do,' Morgan said, 'but that's part of the joy. It's worst at the beginning though.'

I looked confused.

'The first day is wonderful. After a couple of hours, I feel so horny, it's wonderful,' he said. 'I just want my ass to open and be filled ... with anything, a cock, a huge dildo, a fist ....'

He was smiling beautifully.

'Then, day two is harder,' he went on, 'towards the evening and night. You're so conscious of it that it's real anger-making. I just want to try and tear it off. Then, once you've got to sleep, from day three on, I'm just so horny and obedient it's wonderful. Some guys say that it takes a week or two before they settle down in them. They think it takes that long for their bodies to get used to higher testosterone levels. They even get short-tempered and irritable, a bit like the start of roid rage. It's best letting those around have some idea of what you're doing if that's going to happen.'

'So when, if you don't mind me asking, did you last come?' I said, hoping I wasn't been too personal.

'Not, in the least,' Morgan said, confidently. 'I'm proud of it. Nearly two months ago now.'

I gasped.

'Two months? Wow,' I said. 'I find two days without jerking off difficult, sometimes two hours.'

'You'll learn,' Peter said behind me.

For a moment, I wondered what I was letting myself in for.

'How do you keep clean?' I asked, turning my attention back to Morgan.

'In a word,' he said, 'carefully. I have to bath or take the shower head and spray it round me very precisely to make sure that everywhere is clean.'

I nodded.

'Then,' he said, 'and this is the most ridiculous aspect of it, I have to use a hair-dryer!'

I shook my head. It was hard to believe.

'Oh, and because I'm cut, it's easier,' Morgan said. 'It's far harder for people with foreskins to make sure they're really clean. If I have a bath I know water can get into the tube more easily than in a shower. Sometimes the Master will let me out while I am here and wash while I clean myself and shave. Then he will lock me in again.'

I shuddered. It was both beautiful and almost too much for me. Morgan caught my reaction.

'There are bonuses,' he said.

'Really?' I asked, intrigued.

'Yes,' he said. 'It's a lot easier than a cup jock. You have no choice whatsoever about touching yourself. It really does help you keep your focus on the Master.'

'You'll find out,' Peter said.

'I'm not entirely sure I want to,' I said.

'It won't be for a while, you can relax,' Peter said. 'They're expensive and the Master won't invest in one for you until he's really sure that you'll be spending quite a lot of time with us.'

'That's true,' Morgan added. 'And, I'm only spending more time in this as I have to be away so often. The Master thinks that I am more dedicated as a result. I think he's right in that too.'

Peter caught me a knowing expression.

'He probably thought you'd been doing something you shouldn't have been,' he said to Morgan.

'I wish,' Morgan said, laughing.

I'd spent so much time with my attention on the metal belt that I'd almost failed to appreciate his wonderful body. He was a good few inches taller than me, around six foot. His chest was broad and well defined. His abdominal muscles too were clearly marked. His butt was round, his thighs strong and his calves well developed too.

'May I?' I asked as I ran my hand towards his thigh. 'Only for a second,' Morgan said.

I was astonished by the texture. I could feel the hair beginning to grow. It was short and tough. I hadn't realized until then that almost his entire body was devoid of hair. I couldn't see entirely behind the plate of the belt, but I suspected that there would be little if any hair there either.

'Stubble,' I said, surprised.

'Of course,' Morgan said. 'I shave most weeks.'

'So,' said Peter from behind us, 'do I.'

I felt Peter's remark was pointed. I turned and looked at him.

'And, so, probably very soon will you,' he added, grinning at me.

'Don't worry,' Morgan said. 'You learn very quickly. There's a knack, so you don't cut yourself, and if you do it regularly, then you don't have the problems or the soreness that can occur when it grows back.'

I must have looked unconvinced.

'And,' Peter said, 'it feels wonderful.'

Morgan grinned. 'Yes, there's something about a breeze on newly- shaven skin ... .'

I could see a far-away look in his eyes. I wondered where

his imagination had taken him.

I looked them both up and down. They were truly magnificent specimens. Peter was like a terrier, small and defined. Morgan was taller, thicker set, an athlete certainly, but not a heavy football player. I felt gross in comparison.

Morgan noticed my admiration.

'He likes what he sees,' he said to Peter.

'He's got room to improve,' Peter said, 'and he will. We'll see to that.' He smirked.

I only saw the chain locked around Morgan's right ankle as he sat down. I knew Peter had one, but I also noticed for the first time that both men had small tattoos on their ankles too, just below the bone.

I reached forward to look at Morgan's more closely.

'We all have one,' he said. 'When the Master accepts us permanently.'

He held up his foot for me to see the decoration more closely. It was a very simple monogram.

'The Master's,' he said.

It was enough.

'Are you ready?' Peter said.

I wondered what he was talking about.

'For what?' I said.

'To go.'

My face fell.

'If I must.'

'It's about time. There are just a couple of things.'

'Yes?' I said.

'Firstly, your clothes are in our downstairs closet. Go and get dressed, you may shower if you want, and then come back here.'

As I left the room, I could just hear the two others talking.

'He's nice,' Morgan said.

'He has potential', Peter replied.

I decided against a shower. I would have a long hot soak in a bath when I got home, even if it meant wearing a damp jockstrap for a while. I knew that I'd have a lot to think about and the relaxation would do me good. I didn't know, not now, quite how long it would be before I had a chance for another.

I pulled on my jeans. They pushed the cup jock into me tightly. I hoped I wouldn't be too distracted on the drive home. I picked up my keys and wallet from beside the washbasin. I went back to the kitchen.

Peter looked at me disapprovingly.

'You look like a bar slut,' he said.

I felt dismayed. I thought I looked good in a tight white tee-shirt, jeans and boots.

'When you come next, you will wear proper clothes,' he said, deliberately emphasizing the word proper, 'including a tie. I know it's what Mr Woods ordered, but this is my domain now.'

'Yes, Peter,' I said. I'd almost called him 'Sir'.

'As it's your first visit, you're excused,' he said, grinning.

'Thank you,' I said. There were almost tears of disappointment in my eyes.

Morgan noticed.

'Don't worry,' he said. 'Peter is a real stickler for formality and convention, but his bark's worse than his bite.'

I wondered. I also wondered what it would be like coming to the Master's house dressed more formally. I associated sex with jeans and leather, dressing down more than dressing up.

'Come here,' Peter was in command once again. I obeyed.

'Drop your jeans.'

I stood in front of him and undid the button fly. I pushed the denim down over my fly.

'And the jock,' he said.

I pushed it down. Although I'd been almost naked in front of Peter for most of the day, I felt awkward being in this position in front of him. He looked down at my growing cock.

'You'll get used to that,' he said, referring to the approaching erection, 'and not being able to do anything about it.'

I heard Morgan snigger behind me.

'Here,' Peter said, 'put this on.'

He handed me what I thought was a rubber cockring. However, when I touched it there was an elasticity greater than normal rubber.

Peter noticed my curiosity.

'Neoprene,' he said, 'what wet suits are made from.'

I pulled my balls through the ring, the right one, which was slightly larger, first. I closed my eyes and tried to concentrate on nothing for a few moments; it was the only way I could get my erection to subside enough to get the ring into place. It took a while. It would have taken far longer if the ring hadn't been so easy to stretch. It felt good when it was in place.

'It looks good,' Peter said when I had finished adjusting it. He pulled the jockstrap up over my buttocks, but pulled the pouch forward.

He let it snap back into place.

'Ow,' I said, as I reached down to rescue my balls and place them inside the pouch properly.

'You enjoyed that,' I said accusingly to Peter as I reached to pull my jeans up.

'A little perk,' Peter said, smiling mischievously. 'I make the most of them when I can.'

'You can be sure of that,' Morgan added.

I thought I had finished when I had done up the button fly, but no.

'Lift your right leg and pull up your jeans,' Peter said.

It was only as I was doing as I was told that I noticed the

chain in his hands. I struggled to keep my balance as he wound the chain round my leg, reached for a small padlock and snapped it into place. I could feel my erection getting firmer as he did.

I took a deep breath. The action had almost made me cum. Peter nodded and I put my leg back down. I was pleasantly surprised when he grasped my shoulders and kissed me on the lips.

'Welcome,' he said.

He turned me. I hadn't noticed that Morgan had walked across to us. He too grasped and bent to kiss me gently and lovingly.

'You have started a journey, young man,' he said. 'You already know yourself far better than many of the people you will pass as you go back to where you live. You have grown. You have discovered and acknowledged a vital and essential part of the man that is you. You have already done far more in your life than many. Be pleased in that. Be proud.'

'But do not,' Peter said, taking up this liturgy, 'be complacent, because complacency comes before a fall.'

I nodded and kissed Morgan back. It was hard not to lust after him and his beautiful lithe, restrained, constrained, body.

'You may have started a journey,' Peter continued, 'but remember that this is only the start. The journey is a long one, and hard. But it is the only one you have. It is the journey to fulfilment, the real, most important, you.'

I nodded. 'Thank you,' I said.

'Now, be away with you, until Friday. You will contact me tomorrow, won't you?'

'Yes, Peter,' I said, 'I will.'

Brian's support

The drive back to the apartment was a challenge. I really had to concentrate hard on the road. My mind was trying to run through everything that had happened to me in the previous twenty-four hours. I felt tired. I felt elated. I could feel my cock getting hard in my jock. I had to fight to pay attention to the other traffic.

The journey can't have taken me more than about an hour, but it felt a lifetime. The transition from the world that was the house and home of my Master – my Master, even that didn't feel quite right or real – to driving myself in my beaten-up, used, budget hatchback and my new apartment was strange. I suddenly appreciated what Peter meant about dressing properly.

There was something beautiful about the formality of the Master's household. No one was taken for granted. The ritual prevented that. He didn't just assume you were doing something, he knew where you were, especially when you were in the same room, because he had had to acknowledge your knock on the door, give you permission to approach him. There was a dignity too. Yes, I thought, Peter was right, very right, jeans and tee-shirts were for the bars, not a home, and certainly not that sort of home.

My roommate Brian was in when I got to the apartment. I was glad there was life in the place, but at the same time resented his presence. I wanted time, space, on my own to think through what had happened, what was happening. Mom had been shocked by the speed with which I'd made the announcement and then taken my things. Dad had known better. He recognized escape when he saw it. I'd caught his eye when I told them. I could have sworn that for an instant he was jealous. He'd looked away so quickly that I was fairly sure I'd been party to a guilty secret.

Now, I'd run into another irony; the freedom of the apartment at the same time as I'd accepted the constraints of Mr Woods' household. This, I thought, had at least been my own, free choice, not an obligation of family life, forced unwillingly on me.

'Have a good time?' Brian called as I took the bag containing my work suit into my bedroom.

'Yeh, great,' I called back non-committally. 'I'm going to have a bath.'

I unpacked my suit and put it on a hanger to let any creases fall out while the bathwater was running.

I slowly climbed out of my jeans and tee-shirt. I stood, letting the air caress my naked butt, but simultaneously looking at the bulge of the cup jock in a mirror.

Speedos, I remembered the Master saying, and a cup jock at night. I opened a draw. I looked at my small collection. It took me a moment to realize that since earlier that day they were no longer really mine. I pulled the items out and placed them carefully on my bed. Where once I would have thrown them across the room, I now carried them delicately.

I looked at the clock beside my bed. It was nearly 7pm. There was no way I would be going out that evening. After my bath, I thought, I'll slip into some sweat pants, have something to eat, and then enjoy a glass of wine. Starting the Speedo regime now might be a little much.

No one would know about the extra layer of clothing. If there was nothing on TV to catch my attention, I'd read. No, I thought, I would write out my list for Peter.

I suppose, I thought, that I should wear something in the bath now. My cock was supposed to be 'off limits'. I pulled two Speedos from the small pile. There was a plain blue pair that I'd bought in Paris and a patterned pair that had cost me all of a dollar in a thrift store in Chicago's boyztown the year before; several times I'd enjoyed lying on a beach trying to dream which 32-inch waist stud had worn them before me. I put them on.

I walked through to the bathroom. I added some foam to the running water before I got in. The warmth felt wonderful. I laid back and relaxed. It felt a little unusual, wearing Speedos in the bath. I'll take them down to wash myself, I thought. I looked down at the bulge within them. They were tight, but felt good.

'Wine?' Brian, my roommate called.

'Yes, please,' I replied. That certainly would be a treat.

It was a few moments before there was a knock on the door and he came in. I didn't have time to say anything before he was putting a glass down on a shelf beside the bath for me. He had one himself. He looked me up and down. I liked the attention.

'Speedos in the bath?' Brian said. 'Kinky.'

'Yes,' I said, 'I suppose it is.'

He looked at me knowingly.

'There must be a reason,' he said.

He was fishing for more. I wondered how much I should tell him.

He saved me the trouble.

'For your benefit or someone else's?' he asked.

'Someone else's,' I admitted.

Brian sat down on the toilet seat. 'Orders?'

'How do you know?' I asked.

Brian raised his eyebrows knowingly. He smiled, taking his time before answering.

'Let's just say I know,' he said.

'Will you tell me sometime?' I asked, hoping for more.

'Probably, but I want to know more about you, first,' he said. 'Let me guess, you're not allowed to touch or play with yourself?' I nodded.

Brian reached into the bath and patted his hand against my cock and balls. The reaction was instantaneous; my cock started to swell. At any other time, I would have be righteously indignant. Instead, I passively accepted his attention.

'A cockring too,' he said. 'His?'

'Yes,' I said, 'it's his.'

'Um,' Brian said, looking at me enviously. 'So, Jimmy, just how much are you going to tell me?'

If he knows this much, I thought, he might as well know it all. I started to tell him about the previous day, and the run-up to it.

The bathwater was getting cold when I finished and my wine glass was empty. I stood up.

Brian reached for a towel and started to dry me. He patted the pouch of the Speedos carefully and firmly, letting the towel absorb as much of the water as it could.

'You've been here too,' I said, suddenly alerted by his behavior that the attention and interest was more than mere curiosity.

Brian looked up at me and smiled.

'That could be good, it could be bad,' he said.

I looked puzzled. I hadn't realized.

'I can hold you hand through the easy bits and then be your conscience when some things don't seem quite so appealing,' he said, knowingly.

Although we had agreed that our individual bedrooms in the apartment would be private, I let him follow me into mine. He immediately noticed the cup jock on the bed and smiled.

'I have an idea,' he said. 'You said you're not allowed to touch yourself, right?'

'Correct,' I said, 'I'm not.'

'And, these?' he said, picking up the blue Speedos.

'For now,' I said.

'Stand still and lift you hands above your head,' Brian said. I did as he instructed.

From behind, he reached around my waist and undid the cord of the Speedos. He pulled them down. I stepped out of them. He took the towel and dried between the cheeks of my ass and between my legs from the back. I could feel my cock getting hard again. He reached round me and very gently and sensuously took my balls in his hands. He tried to get the towel under the cockring and dry me as carefully and as fully as possible. My erection was complete by the time he stopped.

He put the blue Speedos on the floor. I stepped in to them. He looked me in the eye as he bent and pulled them up my legs. He arranged my balls before stepping behind me to tie the waist cord.

'There,' he said, 'you didn't touch yourself.'

He bent forward and cheekily kissed my erection through the tight material.

'Thank you,' I said. The sensation felt delicious. The Master hadn't said that I shouldn't come, I thought, only that I shouldn't touch myself. I wondered if I would be able to hump my bed while wearing a cup jock enough to make me.

'What other orders do you have?' Brian asked.

I told him.

'I'm going to enjoy this,' he said. 'I'll be back in a second.'

I was wondering what he was going to do when he came back into my room with a pad and a pen.

'You write,' he said, 'and I'll call everything out. I'll make sure you don't cheat.'

It took us an hour, but we did it. Brian was exceedingly thorough. He made me open every drawer for him. Everything, yes, everything, was listed by the time we'd finished. We had had some more wine, but we'd continued working on the list at the same time.

'You have a nice collection,' he said.

'Thanks,' I said, 'but it's no longer really mine.' Brian smiled.

'There's quite a lot too,' he said.

I wasn't sure whether I should be embarrassed. I still felt a little uncomfortable about admitting my fetish for underwear.

'You have good taste,' Brian said.

'Some were gifts,' I said, bashfully.

'That's nice,' he said.

'And, your Master?' Brian said.

'I think he likes underwear too,' I said. 'He certainly likes jockstraps, and one of his slaves, his boys, is locked into a metal chastity belt.'

'Really?' Brian said, clearly fascinated. 'I had to wear one of those once.'

'Only once?' I teased.

'Yes, only once,' he said, his disappointment showing.

'I didn't know you had such interests,' I said.

'You didn't ask.'

'I suppose not,' I said. My listing for a roommate has specified only that I was looking for another gay male, not someone kinky. Brian's revelations were becoming a welcome bonus.

'What happened?' I said.

'He died,' Brian said, 'a brain tumor. He was only forty-three.'

I reached for his hand.

'I am sorry,' I said. He was trying hard to hold back the tears. 'You clearly loved him very much,' I said.

'He was very special,' Brian said, 'very special indeed.' He wiped the tears from the corner of his eyes.

'You're lucky, Jimmy,' he said. 'You seem to have found someone really good.'

'I could introduce you?' I said, hoping that I wasn't rushing ahead too far or too quickly.

'I don't think that would be a good idea,' he said, 'it's still too recent, but thank you, I do appreciate it.'

He squeezed my hand.

'He was into underwear too,' Brian said, 'but in a different way.'

'Yes,' I said, hoping he would tell me more.

He took my hint.

'He only liked one style, a particular white brief, so that was all that was allowed. Everything had to be white. I was allowed one jockstrap and one pair of Speedos too, but they both had to be white.'

He shrugged. 'They were comfortable, but it took me a while not to miss the variety. I was sometimes allowed to wear white shorts in the house. Sportswear had to be white too. Tanktops, shorts, socks, shoes, sweat pants; he would inspect me regularly to make sure everything was spotless.'

'I understand,' I said, reaching for his hand again. 'I bet you looked good.'

'I like to think so,' he said. 'That sounds like me.'

'When he had visitors, I had to wear a jock, tight white sports shorts, T-shirt or tanktop, white socks and shoes. He liked my hair cropped short too. I felt good in it,' he said, before falling silent.

I let him remember. It was a while before he spoke.

'Do you want me to help?' he said.

'I think that would be nice,' I said, 'but it scares me a little.'

'You should let your Master know I have made the offer,' he said.

'I will do that,' I said, 'but what do you have in mind?'

'I'll check that you're doing what you said you'll do,' Brian said, 'or I can check to make sure you're fulfilling your orders. Nothing more, nothing less. I know there are temptations, Jimmy, I've been there too remember.'

There was something beautifully close between us at that moment, sitting together on my bed, wine glasses to hand. I was naked apart from the Speedos and cockring. Brian was in a light gray tee-shirt and jeans. He looked good.

I hadn't really thought about him too much. He'd called the day after my classified advertisement had appeared in the local gay newspaper.

Getting the apartment had been a pleasant surprise. One of the executives at work had been offered an attachment to the company's Atlanta office. They wanted someone for a year. It was just the excuse I wanted. I didn't have to tell Mom I was moving out permanently. I'd been asked to do a friend, a colleague, a favor and look after their home. It was only temporary, Mom, I'll be back before long. You won't even have had time to notice I'm gone. Dad had winked knowingly, conspiratorially.

Only it wasn't quite like that. There was rent to pay. There were bills to cover. I wouldn't be able to afford it on my own. Sheila, my colleague and the apartment's owner, said she wouldn't mind me sharing, but I would be responsible. I accepted her offer. I'd placed the advert within an hour of our deal being done.

Brian was the second person to come and look at the apartment.

My co-worker Sheila let me have some keys even though I hadn't moved in and she hadn't moved out. We went through everything in a hurry. Everything I didn't want or need would be stored by her sister; she had a big house with big stables, a big family and several big Labrador retriever dogs in the country. If I needed space during the time I was there, I only had to make sure that whatever was Sheila's was taken there. I couldn't complain.

Brian brought references with him. I called and checked them out while he was there. He'd offered a cash deposit and had seemed sensible enough. He was three years older than me, and working as a trainee manager in a travel company. He was fit, clean-shaven and good-looking. I felt I could cope with looking at him across the cereal and coffee each morning. He'd also said he was neat, tidy and could clean and cook. I thought we'd be able to get along well together. We'd agreed at that first meeting that we wouldn't, really, try to poach each other's conquests. We would admire where appropriate, we'd said, but not touch unless invited. It seemed a reasonable enough arrangement.

I was even more pleased when a set of weights arrived when he moved in. I'd told him he could leave them in the sitting room we shared if he didn't mind me using them. The only stipulation he'd made was that he'd like to watch sometime. I was beginning to understand why.

So, there it was. Sheila moved everything out to her sister's on the Wednesday. Brian and I took over on the Thursday. My father delivered more of my things on Friday. I'd be out that night but back on Saturday, sometime. I'd wondered whether to call off the Master's arrangement. I didn't. That so many changes were happening at once felt like life taking me firmly in a new direction. I could have fought that, but I felt more comfortable going with it. I felt that seeing the

Master would be a reward at the end of a frantic week. If I'd moved any earlier, I doubt that I would have ever replied to the Master's listing. The frustrations of the parental home had been the incentive I'd needed.

That first Thursday evening, there had been some animal-like sniffing around one another. About nine, one of Brian's friends had called, another good-looking guy called Ian. We spoke, but the conversation was formal and a little strained, as if Ian was an ex- boyfriend with a legacy of jealousy that hadn't burned itself out. I was quite pleased when, after spending ten minutes or quarter of an hour in Brian's room, they'd gone out.

I think we intended to keep our lives separate. We did our own laundry and our own dishes that first evening. I didn't like that; it seemed a little wasteful for him to clear up when I'd have pots and pans to wash a few minutes later. Similarly, it seemed extravagant for us each to run a washing machine and tumble drier half full. It irked. A chance phone call, asking him to be in work early the next morning gave me the excuse I needed. I told him I'd take care of his laundry, load the machine. Don't, he had said, let any colors run.

I need not have worried; everything he'd put out was white. I resisted temptation too. I didn't rub my nose in his underwear as I carefully loaded the shirts, tee-shirts and a single jockstrap into the machine. He came home as I was hanging the underwear and socks on a drying frame in the bathroom. Tumble dryers can ruin waistbands, I'd told him. He noticed, but said nothing, when I ironed his shirts and tee-shirts along with my own.

I'd told him then that I didn't expect to be home on Friday and that it might well be Sunday morning before I reappeared. It was when he took his clean clothes that I first noticed that look in his eye. It seemed distant, regretful, a recollection of times past. I didn't understand it. I reached for his hand. He let me hold him.

'I think we could become good friends,' I said.

'So,' Brian answered, 'do I.'

He paused.

'Now,' he said, 'tell me, what are your instructions for the week?'

Sunday, Monday

Sunday had passed quietly. In the morning, I had slipped on some sweat pants before going out for the newspaper. Even then, I'd been wondering who might have noticed the strange protrusion. There were a few people about, so I had held the bundle of Sunday sections strategically in front as I walked the few hundred yards back to the apartment.

It was one of those Sundays where there was actually quite a lot I'd wanted to read. The morning had passed quickly. Brian had gone out, when work called, but we hadn't said much. In the afternoon, I did something I hadn't done for a long time; I started writing letters. When he came back in the late afternoon, Brian had typed the list for me. It was only, I told him, so he knew what I had. The sheets would be clearer to fax to Peter than my handwriting.

It was only when another friend called to say he was on his way round for coffee that I finally showered and got dressed. I'm sure he must have wondered what was going on. I'm not sure why, but the cup jock felt uncomfortable under the jeans I had chosen. Sitting down on the settee was awkward; it felt as if I was crushing myself a little too much. So, for the hour or so we spent talking, I sat on the mat in front of the fire. I tried to make it seem as relaxed and natural as I could, but I don't think I did too well. Although we were close friends, I was glad when he went.

Brian was watching when I went early to bed.

* * *

I was woken by the sound of the knock on the door.

'Come in,' I said, trying to rub my eyes, turn on the light and wake up, all at the same time.

It was Brian. He had a mug of coffee in one hand and a letter in the other.

'I thought you might like this,' he said, putting the coffee mug down on the nightstand beside my bed.

'And this came too,' he added, handing me the letter.

It was personal and had a London postmark. I didn't recognize the writing. I wondered who it was from. Inside, there was a postcard, elegantly embossed with the Master's address.

'I forgot, boy,' the message said, 'to tell you one thing: You will only be permitted to have sex elsewhere with express permission and you will have to telephone your Master each time.'

I showed it to Brian.

'I must admit I wondered,' he said. 'Nice. It's good that he's thinking of you.'

'But no sex,' I said.

'No sex.' Brian grinned. 'How's that cup this morning?'

'Okay,' I said, remembering the jockstrap. I had expected it to be harder getting to sleep than it had been. I had been so tired that I hadn't even had the energy to try to hump a pillow. It had taken me a little while to find a position that was comfortable, where the cup didn't press into me and keep me awake, but I hadn't woken at all during the night. I was pleasantly surprised.

'I have taken a liberty,' Brian said.

I looked up at him, wondering what he could have done.

'Yes,' I said, cautiously.

'Well,' he said, 'I haven't done it quite yet. It's really something that I'd like to ask you and that I'd like you to do.'

I looked at him. I took a sip of coffee before responding. 'Well?'

'If I remember correctly, from our conversation last night,

today should be your last day for choosing what you could wear yourself.'

'Yes,' I said. 'It is.'

'I thought you may like these,' he said, bringing a skimpy white bikini brief out from behind his back.

'I do,' I said. They looked a high quality. I couldn't see a designer waistband, but the material had a sheen to it. I tried to reach out for them, but Brian held them away from me.

'Not so fast,' he said. 'They were bought for me ....'

I stopped, suddenly appreciating the broader significance of what he was saying.

'Yes,' I said. 'I understand.'

'I only have one pair left after these.'

'You shouldn't then,' I said.

'Yes,' Brian said, slowly and definitely, 'I should. I think it is appropriate.'

'You realize I will have to "declare" them?' I said, 'and add them to the household.'

'That's what convinced me,' he said. 'I don't think many people would understand, but they were bought as a token that signified what I was doing at the time. It seems right that a such a token should again find a place in such a ritual.'

'I understand,' I said.

'It's almost as if what they are is incidental,' Brian said. 'It could have been a ring, or a collar, or a leather thong. I want to give you something to wish you well on your journey of exploration.'

I leant forward and kissed his knee.

'Thank you,' I said.

He leant too, kissing my forehead before he turned and left the room.

'I'll see you tonight,' he called. A moment later, I heard the front door shutting behind him.

* * *

I took the briefs and held them to my nose. They smelled clean. I couldn't help but wonder whether, as well as Brian, his Master had worn them.

I thought of another friend, in the United States, with a fetish for underwear too. He would trade items with friends around the world, some new, some worn, a few very well worn. He liked to know an item's history, he called it the 'provenance'. Much as I tried, I couldn't imagine some of the world's great auction houses publishing catalogues of endlines of Calvin Klein underwear, let alone descriptions of those who had bought and worn it. Still, if he could, he would try to get a photograph of the items being worn. He didn't need to see the face, he said, just the body, especially if it was a nice body.

I wondered if I would ever find out more about the history of these briefs and their significance from Brian. He had told me about some aspects of his own life and background the previous evening, but I'd felt distinctly as if I would be told what he thought I should know when he was ready to tell me. Some questions I had asked had been ignored. Others had been answered only partially or obliquely. I had a feeling that I would be told more and more of the story, but only in Brian's own time. Frustratedly curious, I knew I would have to wait.

I showered wearing the cup jock. It was soaked before I took it off. It was the last task I performed. I took the cockring off for a moment too, and rinsed it. After drying, I dusted my cock and balls with a light covering of talc before I put it back. I lifted Brian's white briefs and respectfully kissed the pouch and the butt before putting them on.

I stood there naked apart from the briefs for a few moments, looking at myself in the full-length mirror. The narrow pouch held my cock up against my belly and supported my balls almost as if they were in a small cup. I had to admit that it looked good. It felt good too. My cock was hardening again as I pulled on my chinos.

I was sorely tempted to show off mercilessly that morning, but I restrained myself. It was only the thought that the Master may not want to be represented by an exhibitionist strumpet that stopped me. So, instead of my customary polo, I chose a plain blue Oxford shirt and tie.

I had to shake my head a couple of times as I walked to catch the train. It was nice not to have to drive to work. I liked that change too. It would be healthier, cheaper and less frustrating than sitting in morning traffic jams. I felt as if I was walking about two feet off the ground as I headed towards the train station. The sun was shining and the world seemed full of good-looking men. The mailman's butt seemed rounder than I had remembered and there was an interesting bulge in the front of his uniform trousers. He wasn't wearing boxers, I thought. There was a guy starting construction work whose jeans looked exceedingly well filled, and whose butt looked wonderfully round. I wasn't hard, but I could feel the cock filling, trapped inside the white briefs. If either of the guys had beckoned me to them and said 'kneel', I probably would have done so.

My newspaper remained unread on the train. My eyes were everywhere else. I was even looking at older businessmen in shiny, frayed suits. I was trying to imagine them in leather or denim, standing with beers in their hands at a bar. Some, I decided, were not unattractive. There were some strong faces. With shorter hair, and losing some weight, a few could have been quite hot.

I was really pleased that the day in the office was busy. My boss, David, wanted this doing, and that, and three other things, all at the same time and all of them should have been completed and delivered to clients by the end of the previous week. At least, that's how it felt.

'Hey, Jimmy,' he said, finally, as lunchtime approached, 'you look happy today.' It was good of him to notice, I thought, as I looked up from the latest pile of paper.

'Thank you,' I said, just stopping myself in time from adding 'Sir.' That would either have been plainly inappropriate or provoked far too many questions.

'You look good too,' he said. I grimaced, I didn't really want to remember at that very minute that I was wearing a cockring and it was Thursday since I'd last come.

'Thanks,' I said, turning and trying to leave his office.

'A good weekend?' asked David, clearly probing, trying to find out as much as he could pry out of me.

'Yes, thank you, David,' I said, hoping that this wasn't the start of a long, informal, lunchtime conversation.

'Good, you can tell me more about it another time,' he said, 'I have to go out. I'm meeting Sylvia for lunch.'

I sighed with relief. Such comments made me think about people. I wondered just how much they could cope with an honest answer. Could David really understand if I'd told him I had spent an evening in chains in an attic, sexually servicing another man, and that I had spent the following day around his house wearing only a jockstrap? I honestly didn't know.

I sat down at my desk and grinned. I'd met David's wife, Elaine. She was elegant, handsome even, and spent most of her time being a lady-who-lunched or doing things charitable for a golf or country club in Connecticut. She'd promise prizes for raffles and competitions which we, I, would then have to cajole from our clients. Did they dress up in black latex, I wondered. I tapped my fingers on the desk. Yes, I thought, there's just that sparkle of wickedness in Elaine's eyes. I could picture her, top-to-toe in leather, high, and I mean high, heels and a riding crop, held in one hand and being tapped on the other. Could I see David on his knees at her feet? No, somehow I couldn't. My mental picture was of him taking off his jacket and saying 'you do what you want, dear, I'll just have a cup of tea.'

I wanted it to be one o'clock. I didn't want it to be. I tried to leave for my break as nonchalantly as I could. I didn't want to give the impression that I was in a hurry. I hoped the exercise wouldn't take long. I had already addressed an envelope and found a plain white postcard. In fact, I'd done that within about half an hour of getting in to work. I'd even written it.

'As ordered, Sir,' I'd said. 'In anticipation of Friday, respectfully, Jimmy.' I'd wondered about adding 'your slave', but felt that was perhaps too presumptuous. I'd been told I was on trial. 'Your prospective slave?' I wondered. If in doubt, I remembered, do without.

I had the card and envelope in my pocket. I hoped they wouldn't get too creased. I also had Mr Woods' cash. Not only did I have to get the ordered items, I had to buy a stamp and post the receipt. Michelle at reception noticed as I went to leave the building.

'You don't usually go out on a Monday, Jimmy,' she said. I thought fast.

'I have to get to the Post Office,' I said, 'I need to get this in the mail. It's due by tomorrow.'

I hoped she'd accept the excuse and not remember that I usually sent the gas bill, like everyone else did if they'd lost the reply-paid envelopes, to be franked in the company mail room. David had asked me to send his off one time, and then told me to send my payments that way too. Michelle said nothing. I relaxed as I turned into the street. I looked at my watch. It was just after one. I would have to hurry. I knew I could have gone after work, but I wouldn't have got to the Post Office before it shut.

I wanted to keep Mr Woods' note. I almost felt like framing it. I felt caught. There was no way, that month, after moving into the flat, that I could afford to spend much on swimwear, however much I was tempted.

I nipped in and out of the crowds. I'd seen the garments that Mr Woods wanted in a sports store the week before. If it hadn't been for the moving expenses, there would already have been one, perhaps two, in my collection.

They were still there when I got there. The store wasn't too busy either. I noticed again the duty security guard. There was one local contractor who seemed to have won the business of all the stores in the area. The uniforms were cut nicely and the men all seemed young. The beige material hugged their thighs and buttocks. There was no room for anything in the pockets.

I could see the young man watching me as I bent to the rail where the square cut items were hanging. I felt that he could remember me; I'd done almost exactly the same a week earlier. I was glad the money burning a hole in my pockets had come from Mr Woods.

There were only two styles. Both were black and one had an orange stripe down the side, the other bright green. It was tempting to select the size thirties. If I'd been buying solely for myself, I may well have bought one of them that much tighter, but I remembered in time that Peter, Morgan, perhaps even Mr Woods himself may wear these too. The thirty-two waist size would probably be better. I smiled. Shopping had suddenly become a shared, collective experience. What would the security guard have thought, I wondered, as I picked them off the rail?

Even grinning, I felt my face was turning red as I took the two items to the cash desk. The guard was there too now, talking to the woman behind the counter. She ignored me as she recorded the barcodes from the labels and put the shorts into a bag. I had had to add some of my own money to Mr Woods' note. The woman tried to put the receipt into the bag as she handed me a few coins as change. I took it from her separately.

I tucked the bag under my arm as I left the store. As I went passed the window, I could see the security guard looking in my direction. He seemed to be ignoring the woman's conversation.

If I hadn't been in such a hurry, I might have slowed down and cruised him. And, I might also have done it if I felt I hadn't made a commitment to Mr Woods. I remembered the envelope. That too was in my pocket. As I ducked and weaved through the lunchtime shoppers towards the Post Office, I thought about a possible telephone call.

I did think I would have the chutzpah to call Mr Woods and say: 'I've picked up a security guard in a sportswear store Sir, please may I shag him?'

I could however imagine Mr Woods telling me to go to the store and offer the guard my services; that was another scenario altogether. The Post Office was busy when I got there. I tucked the receipt into the envelope and kissed it as I sealed it. I had no option but to slow down and think as I waited in line. I wondered about the shorts in the bag. Mr Woods had said put them on tomorrow. I wondered if I could try them this evening. Brian knew about them. I laughed to myself. Mr Woods had told me to buy them because I'd told him that I didn't think Brian would appreciate me running round the apartment dressed only in Speedo briefs. Now I knew that, if anything, Brian would like me in the briefs more than the square-cut style. Ah well, I thought, there's nothing I can about it now.

Even though David was out, and as he was lunching with Sylvia he would probably wouldn't be back at all that day, I still hurried back to the office.

'Get the envelope in the mail then?' Michelle asked as I pressed the security entry keys.

'Yes thanks,' I said, not wanting to add anything.

'And a present?' she asked, peering at the bag under my arm. 'That's right,' I lied, 'something for my brother. It's his birthday this week.'

'I didn't know you had a brother,' Michelle said as the door closed behind me.

I don't, I thought, but it was the only excuse I could think of. Could Michelle have coped with the truth? I've been buying swimwear because another man wants me to wear it in my own apartment. Michelle might come in some mornings looking as if she had come straight from a club, without having slept, making appreciative noises about male teenagers who'd been dancing in boxer shorts, but the truth and relative sobriety might have been hoping for too much.

I went in to the men's room before returning to my own office. I chose a cubicle and took the shorts out of the bag. I held one up. Yes, I thought, they're nice. I hope they'll look as good and feel as good when they are on.

* * *

'I want to see,' Brian said as soon as he walked through the door. I'd laid the two shorts out on my bed.

'They're in my room,' I called from the kitchen.

Brian was sitting on the bed looking at them when I walked in with a mug of coffee for each of us.

'Nice,' he said, 'very nice.'

'I could put them on,' I said.

'No,' Brian responded quickly. 'You're not supposed to put them on until tomorrow morning, are you?'

'No,' I said, hanging my head, 'I'm not.'

'Another delicious torture from your Master,' he teased. 'He's making you wait, making you appreciate, perhaps even enjoy, the anticipation.'

I laughed.

'You'd better get those jeans off,' he said. 'Unless it's really cold, you're not supposed to wear trousers in the flat anymore, are you?'

'No,' I admitted, 'I'm not.'

I started undoing my chinos. I bent to take off my shoes first.

'Trainers,' Brian said. 'They'll do.'

I nodded.

'And a sweatshirt.'

I folded my chinos over a hanger, hung up my tie and put my shirt straight into the laundry basket. Already the Master is making his presence felt, I thought; I'm never usually this tidy at this time. I usually threw things down where they came off and didn't put them away or hang up until bedtime.

I reached for a sweatshirt and my trainers.

As I put my foot down from doing the laces, Brian spoke again. 'Stand still,' he said.

I waited as he looked me up and down.

'You look good like that,' he said, 'very good.'

I sat down on the bed beside him and looked at the shorts again. 'Something to look forward to for the morning,' I said, starting to pick them up.

'Wait,' Brian said. He took one of the Speedos from me. 'You were told that you shouldn't wear these until tomorrow, right?'

'Yes,' I said.

'I have an idea. I don't think your Master will mind too much. And I know you won't.'

I wondered what he was talking about. I waited.

'Stay there,' he said picking up one of the pairs of shorts and leaving my room.

So, I thought, he was going to wear one. Yes, I thought, there were no orders that he shouldn't. I heard him open and close his wardrobe. I waited.

It took him a little longer than I had expected. The vision in my doorway when he reappeared was more than worth waiting for. Brian too was wearing trainers, and a sweatshirt, but a short one that stopped just where the Speedo shorts began. He'd obviously put on a cock ring too. There was the outline of his cock as it pointed upwards and his balls sat comfortably in the pouch.

'Wow,' I said, letting the word out quietly, but more quickly than I would have liked.

'Thank you,' he said. 'It feels good too.'

'It sure does,' I said, in an affected American way. I stood and walked towards him. I kissed him briefly on the lips. Our cocks touched. The sensation felt electric, even inside Brian's white bikini underwear. I jumped back.

'I don't think I should be making telephone calls quite yet,' I said. Brian reached for my hand and squeezed.

'Nor do I.'

A long time in Spandex

Whoever said a week could be a long time in politics obviously hadn't spent anytime forbidden to masturbate and ordered to wear polyester/ spandex swimming shorts for four days.

The Monday evening with Brian had been beautiful and

relaxing. He cooked, making a spaghetti and salad, which we had shared.

He'd also brought in some wine.

'Only one bottle,' he'd said, 'after all, it is only Monday and we both have to get to the weekend.'

There was something wonderfully liberating about wandering around the apartment in the briefs and a sweatshirt.

'I hate to think what the next gas bill will be,' I said as we both sat later, watching the TV news.

'It's only for the occasional evening,' Brian said. 'Tomorrow, it's sweat pants for both of us, despite what your Mr Woods says. He doesn't pay the heating bill.'

It was mind-blowingly romantic. I wanted to hold this man's hand, to caress and kiss him, but at the same time I was starting a commitment to someone that was more structured and more formal. There was a love and great gentleness from Brian; there was the control that Mr Woods had had over Morgan and the more intense sensations I could expect when I saw him on Friday.

Brian noticed when I put my head in my hands.

'You need to be loved, my friend, and you need a framework for your life,' he said. 'We all do.'

I said nothing.

'The structure, the parameters within which we can live, we can exist, even grow,' he said, 'we need those. We also need the love, the strokes ... and the silence.'

I nodded.

'And usually somewhere warm, not just in a cage after we've been beaten,' he said more lightly.

I felt my expression lighten.

'Yes,' I said, quietly and carefully, 'I expect we do.'

* * *

Brian had left the apartment the following morning before I woke. I staggered to the kitchen to make coffee only to find the shorts on the counter. There was a card on top of them.

'Thank you,' it said. 'Don't try looking for the second pair.'

I laughed.

'You randy pervert,' I thought, 'You're breaking in those for me too.'

I had to admit, when I had showered and shaved, that they did feel good to wear. It felt nice knowing that Brian had worn them too. It reminded me of my time in school: if I couldn't have the cock, I'd have the next best thing, literally.

I was happy going to work.

That day, that week, turned into a period of greater activity that I hadn't known for a long time. I tidied my office space. I did more filing. I threw away more old papers. I sent more material to the archive. I actually got the main filing cabinets into alphabetical and numerical order. David's office plants were trimmed and dead leaves removed. Activity, I thought, would be a distraction. It was; and it wasn't.

The mailman and the construction worker became even more good-looking as the week progressed. More and more businessmen on the train were stripped and dressed in leather in my imagination. I had this picture, one morning, of two rows of them, each strap-hanging on the subway, cocks and balls protruding from flies, cod-pieces or chaps, as I worked my way along on my knees, sucking one, then the next and the next until each had come.

I imagined trying to explain that when I arrived at work, admitting how the knees of my chinos had got so filthy, and why there was cum dripping from my chin onto my tie.

I shook my head as I walked along the street towards work. I would have to be careful, I thought. This could get to me. It had certainly got to Brian, I thought when I got home that night. We had a board in the kitchen where we had agreed to list household items that needed buying. So far, it had included really exciting products like 'paper towels' and 'air freshener'. I'd complained about one of Brian's friends smoking when he came into the apartment. Some answer, I'd thought, as I added it to the shopping list.

I did grin when I noticed the table that Brian had drawn on the whiteboard. There were our two names at the top - Jimmy and Brian. At the side were the days of the week – from Monday until Friday. There was nothing under my name for Monday, but under Brian's was the word 'orange' – the swimwear he had 'borrowed' before I'd had a chance to try it on. After that the names and colors alternated. It was clear that he was joining in too. One of his postcards was tucked into the side of the board. I pulled it out.

'You don't mind, do you?' It said. 'I thought it might be fun ... and supportive.'

I wasn't sure. Yes, it was a bit of fun. I hoped it wasn't too much fun. It was supportive, but at the same time, I wanted this to be it. The ritual was mine, for me and for my – potential – Master, Mr Woods. If Brian wanted a master, I thought, he could find one of his own. I was actually a little disappointed when I discovered that he hadn't gone through with it the next morning. I found both pairs hanging on the drier over the bath. They hadn't been washed, just left to air. Seeing them both there surprised and, for a moment, confused me. I couldn't remember which I should be wearing that day; I was glad Brian had put the list on the kitchen board.

I lost track of the days on Wednesday and Thursday. Both seemed awash with sexual images. The pictures of sportsmen in the newspapers seemed to be emphasizing tight butts and well-filled shorts even more than usual. Colleagues suddenly appeared as sexual beings in a way that had never happened before. I even started noticing my female co-workers. I realized that Michelle on reception rarely wore a bra. There was something about Kevin, the company's technical wizard and stereotypically nerdish social bore that I noticed; he seemed very well endowed. If he wore any underwear, it had to be boxers, I thought, noticing the bulge along the inside of his leg as he sat, waiting to see David. I hoped my leering and letching wasn't becoming too obvious. I was beginning to think that whoever had said that men think about sex every five minutes had got it wrong. I thought I was thinking of sex every minute, perhaps every few seconds. I worked with my chair pulled closer to my desk than ever before. The Speedo shorts were pleasantly tight, but I was springing erections so often that I felt someone would notice, probably sooner rather than later. It was so hard, I felt by Thursday, not to run off to the men's room and jack off.

'Brian,' I said that evening, reaching for him and putting my arm around his shoulder. 'I need it so badly.'

He pushed my arm away.

'You can call him', he said. 'Ask for permission.'

'You know I don't want to do that.'

'You may have to,' he said. 'Or will I have to tie your hands behind your back?'

'That won't be necessary,' I said, relaxing a little and smiling.

'It's naughty. You're teasing me and you're enjoying this a little too much ....'

'Well,' he said, 'I can't deny that I am enjoying it, but I don't think too much, really now, do you?'

'I suppose not,' I said reluctantly.

'You're the one who got himself into this position.'

'I know,' I said. 'I suppose if I'd jerked off earlier in the week, he'd never have known. It's too late now.'

'Will he let you come tomorrow?' Brian asked.

'I honestly don't know,' I replied. 'I honestly don't.'

'You'll just have to hope then, won't you?'

He tapped my butt as he went out.

'Don't,' he said, 'do anything I wouldn't do.'

The Run

The letter arrived on Friday morning.

'Bring sweat shirt, pants and trainers,' it said. That was all. It was on one of Mr Woods' embossed cards. It looked like his handwriting. I didn't think it was Peter's.

'What do you think it means?' I asked Brian.

'It could mean that he wants you to be warm,' he replied.

'Thanks,' I said, 'that's really helpful.'

'You may be going for a run,' Brian said. 'You never know. When will you be back?'

'I don't know,' I said, honestly. 'It could be late tonight, tomorrow, Sunday, perhaps even Monday after work.'

'How do you feel?'

'I'm nervous, but as horny as hell,' I said.

'You'll be okay,' Brian said, patting me on the shoulder.

I thought the day would never pass. The trek to work seemed to take longer than ever, but the train was actually on schedule for once. I had a bag packed. I hoped no one would ask me to open it. All it contained was underwear, swimwear and jockstraps. In a section at one end, I'd put the other square cut Speedos and the cup jock. At the other, there were my trainers and sweat pants.

I put the bag as far under my desk as I could. Knowing my luck, it would be the day of a fire drill and we'd all have to leave the building in a hurry.

I needn't have worried. The day was uneventful. I took notes at a meeting in the morning and produced and circulated them in the afternoon. I prepared the papers I needed for Monday. I couldn't wait for four o'clock. I didn't dare leave too soon. That would be too much out of character. I waited, trying to leave casually at about ten minutes past.

'Going away?' Michelle called, as I made my way through the lobby.

'Only for a night or two,' I said.

Once outside the door, I hurried towards the station. It was a longer journey than usual. As I was waiting, I bought a couple of beers from a kiosk. Dutch courage, I thought, as I got onto the train. I arrived early at the Master's house. I rang the bell. Peter let me in. He indicated that I should strip and pointed me towards the room.

'Shower if you want,' he said, 'but keep the jock on.'

He'd remembered. I'd wondered if he would.

'Did you bring everything?'

'I hope so,' I said, pointing to the full bag.

'I got the list. Very thorough,' Peter said.

'My roommate helped,' I said.

Peter looked at me suspiciously, but said nothing. He was looking good. The skimpy light blue swim bikini he was wearing was hardly enough to hold his ample cock and balls, especially with the obligatory cockring. I wanted to bend and kiss the bulge.

'You can look,' he said, appreciating my desire, 'but you know you're not allowed to touch.'

I nodded reluctantly.

'Who is a horny boy then?' Peter teased, running his hand through my hair. I didn't respond. There was no need. I looked at him as defiantly as I could. I didn't do it very well. He shook his head as he left me.

I washed, but didn't shower, and went through to the kitchen.

'Here,' Peter said, handing me a glass of fruit juice. 'The Master is taking you, us, out for a run. Now that the evenings are longer, he thought it seemed a shame to spend it all indoors.'

I nodded.

'We have to be waiting for him at seven,' Peter explained. 'We'll probably go along the river for an hour or so, can you cope with that?'

'I think so,' I said. 'I hope so.'

* * *

At the appointed time, Peter and I were waiting just inside the door of the closet. He'd taken me there to get ready.

'What do you call this place?' I asked.

Peter looked at me surprised.

'Usually something like 'our room',' he said. 'I don't really know, I haven't thought about it that much. The room by the door' perhaps, I don't usually need to say anything. If a boy needs to strip or to shower, he knows where to go. Why do you ask?'

'I was just curious, that was all,' I said. 'I wanted to call it something like the 'servants' closet',' I added.

Peter grinned.

'I suppose it is really,' he said. 'Perhaps may be just The Closet. We're always coming in and out of it, there's a water closet and storage space for our clothes. It makes sense. Perhaps we could.'

We were still grinning when Mr Woods came down the stairs.

I saw his feet first. I gasped when I saw more. He looked amazing. I felt my knees go weak. He was wearing a tight tanktop that showed off his well-defined arms and chest and tight running shorts. They were shiny, just covered his round butt and had a distinct bulge in the front. My mouth fell open.

'You like what you see, Jimmy?' he said, coming and taking hold of my chin.

My hands fell behind my back.

'Yes, Sir, I do, Sir,' I said, bowing my head. It just meant that I was staring even more directly at the bulge in his shorts. I wondered if I could see it getting even bigger.

His response told me he had.

'Be good,' Mr Woods said, 'and you never know, you may get closer to it later.'

He opened the door and led the way out. Peter had some keys in his hand. He locked the door behind us and then led the way to a car. It was an elegant saloon, up-scale but not too ostentatious. He held open one of the doors so Mr Woods could sit in the back. Peter indicated that I should sit in the front beside him. He closed the door once Mr Woods was in.

'You will be doing that soon,' Peter whispered.

There was silence in the car as we drove. I felt a little uneasy, and tried to watch Mr Woods in the back as much as I could. I didn't feel I could be too obvious, so I tried looking in the mirrors. He seemed to be relaxing, looking out of the window, engrossed in his personal thoughts. I wondered what they were.

I was glad it didn't take us long to reach the river. The run was silent too. Mr Woods led the way and Peter and I followed, running side-by-side. We must have looked an interesting trio. Although we didn't speak, Peter and I enjoyed the run. We grinned as we looked down at Mr Woods' butt in front of us. It was a pleasant way to be led on a run, I decided. Mr Woods also had a muscled v-shaped back. It was the first time I had had an opportunity to appreciate it. Peter noticed my focus, smiled and nodded too.

The run was steady, but not too taxing. I hadn't run for a

while and I don't have the natural physique of a runner. I'm short and stocky rather than long-legged and slim, more suited to the gym than jogging. When a past boyfriend had suggested running, I had been reluctant, but lust – then, as now – is a strong motivator for me. I'd even bought some training shoes specially designed for running.

The riverbank was quiet. There were a few people out, walking dogs. We passed three other runners, each alone. Two were in their forties, puffing hard and making determined and not altogether successful endeavors to keep expanding waists under control. The third was young and very attractive. Both Peter and I noticed him. We exchanged appreciative glances. The young man had a physique like Peter's; it was tough and wiry, without any obvious excess body fat. He had close cropped hair. He would have looked wonderful in uniform. He could have been cast as a US Marine in porn, I thought. I was pleased I had Mr Woods butt ahead of me. My attention went back to where it should have been all along.

We were all sweating profusely when we got back to the car. I could see the gleam on Mr Woods' skin. He was giving off such a powerful, wonderful, fresh, masculine aroma too. I wanted to collapse onto his chest and start licking for all I was worth. I hoped I would have a chance. As he sat down in the car, he reached into his shorts to arrange his cock and balls more comfortably. Standing, waiting for Peter to unlock the passenger door for me, I had a perfect view. I had thought that he was wearing a running short with an inner brief, but no, there was a separate Speedo or bikini there. I hoped I would have the honor of a closer inspection when we got home.

Peter reached below his seat and handed Mr Woods a bottle of water. He drank from it before handing it back. Peter drank and then handed it to me. My lust had distracted me from my thirst. I swallowed gratefully.

Peter leaned towards me and whispered as we drew up in front of Mr Woods' home.

'You let him out,' he said, 'I'll open the door.'

As soon as the car had stopped, I was out of my seat belt and round the back of the car to open the door. I stood upright beside it as Mr Woods got out. I hoped that my intense stare at Mr Woods' full shorts wasn't too obvious. I doubted it. He rubbed my hair as he passed me and smiled. I wasn't quite sure what to make of the gesture. I closed the door and followed him towards the house. Peter had opened the door and had moved to one side to let Mr Woods in.

The rituals were formal, like so much of what happened.

'Go in and strip down,' Peter said as I got to the door. 'I'll join you in a second.'

I glanced behind me to see him running to lock the car. I was folding my sweat pants and putting them on top of my training shoes in the small closet when there was a knock on the door. It surprised me.

'Jimmy.' It was Mr Woods' voice. That surprised me even more. It took me a moment to appreciate that he was respecting us and our space by not entering it.

'Yes, Sir,' I responded.

'When you are ready, come out here and kneel,' he said.

'Yes, Sir,' I said, hurrying to fold the clothes neatly. I wondered if I had time for a quick drink of water from the basin. I decided against it. Mr Woods' needs and orders were more important, more immediate. I closed the door behind me quietly. I took two or three paces, enough to let Peter get passed me, and knelt. I closed my eyes. I didn't need sight to know when Mr Woods approached me. I could feel the warmth from his body and the beautiful smell got stronger. He came right up to me. He pressed the bulge in his shorts against my forehead. It felt wonderful. He stood there motionless, letting me drink in the aroma and the situation. No violence was needed, no intense sensation; my submission was complete.

'Yes, Jimmy, you may,' he said, bending so the words were almost whispered into my ear.

'Thank you, Sir,' I said, the words hardly making a sound as they passed my lips.

I raised my head, without opening my eyes, and gently kissed where I could feel his cockhead to be in the shorts. The gesture was not hurried, but I didn't linger either. It was deliberate, but not presumptuous. Then, I bent. I started where his socks met his calves, just above his ankles.

Mr Woods stood still. I felt a muscle tense occasionally as I worked. I attended to one leg as far as the knee and then moved to the other. I shuffled around as I knelt so that I could cover the backs of his legs as well as the front. I took long sweeping licks up his firm muscled calves.

He moved purposefully for the first time when I started to pay attention to his thighs. He moved his legs apart to allow me greater access. It was so tempting to head straight for the ridge between his legs, the perineum between the back of his balls and his ass, where the sweat would probably be greatest. I fought myself and worked each thigh slowly but steadily, sweeping my tongue from his knee to the shorts, straightening my back as I did so.

The Master didn't let me get any higher. He put his hands under my arms, encouraging me to stand. He lifted one of his arms and pushed my head under it. I took the bush of hair into my mouth and started sucking; the fresh perspiration tasting so beautiful. He pushed me away for a second, to pull the tanktop over his head.

Then, again, he stood motionless as I worked to lick every inch of his skin from his neck to the waistband of his shorts. I wasn't sure about licking under his chin until I felt him lift his head back to give me access. I licked his arms too, and each hand, carefully working my tongue between each finger. I never once opened my eyes. Sight would have spoiled the intensity of the other sensations, the touch, the smell, the taste, and the subtle sounds.

It wasn't until I was on my toes, reaching to lick his shoulders that my Speedos brushed the back of his thighs and I realized just how hard my own cock had become. I was suddenly aware that my balls had tightened against the cockring I was wearing inside the shorts. It took hard concentration not to throw my arms around his shoulders and start humping. I screwed up my closed eyes even more as I tried to focus on what I was doing.

The effort, sensations and determination had become so intense that tears appeared at the corners of my eyes in seconds when Mr Woods stepped away from me, leaving me with my mouth open and my tongue hanging out. Even though I was stretching on my toes, I didn't move. After a second or two, I made the most of breathing more easily.

'Come with me,' Mr Woods said.

Cleansing

I opened my eyes, in time to see him starting up the stairs. I hurried to follow. Peter was picking up Mr Woods' tanktop from the floor. His eyes followed as I took the stairs two at a time to catch up.

Mr Woods went into his bathroom. I stopped at the doorway. I let my head fall forward and put my hands behind my back. This was Mr Woods' territory. I knew I was not to enter without express permission.

The Master turned and looked at me. I could see us both in a mirror. We were dressed very similarly. He was wearing tight running shorts. I was in the square-cut Speedos. I had the chain around my ankle. That was the only immediately apparent difference between us. Yet, despite such appearances, our roles were all important. On the riverbank, on a beach, only someone observant enough to notice the ankle chain might have appreciated the dynamic. I took a deep breath. Despite the similarities, he was The Master, I his slave.

'Come in,' said the Master. 'Kneel.'

I took four short steps forward and let myself down as slowly as I could. I didn't want to destroy the pace of what was happening any more. I was about to sit back on my haunches to wait when the Master caught my shoulders and held me, kneeling upright. He placed his shorts in my face.

'Take them off,' he said.

Again, I gently kissed the outline of his cock, and then, separately, each ball. I licked his stomach where it met the waistband as I tried to grasp the material in my teeth. I had to shuffle around, using my arms behind my back to keep my balance, as I pulled the tight garment over his hips. I could feel the briefs over his butt against my cheek as I pulled them down. When the shorts reached his thighs, he pushed me away. They fell to the floor. He stepped out of them and pushed them to one side with one foot. I started to move towards them, to pick them up in my mouth, but he stopped me.

I looked up at him, desire and lust engulfing my gaze. He held my shoulders for a minute. I was almost shivering with excitement. My cock was pushing out my shorts like a tent pole. It was becoming hard to balance.

'Do you realize how beautiful you look?' he said, quietly, in my ear.

I shook my head. Tears were welling up in my eyes. What I

was doing, where I was, felt so right, the emotion was close to overpowering me.

'To have a man where he wants to be, where he needs to be,' Mr Woods said, 'is probably one of the most beautiful sights I know.'

He bent and pushed his hands inside my shorts. I shuddered as his wrist touched my cock. He ignored it as he reached for my balls.

They were so tight against the cockring that he could get them both in one hand. He started squeezing. I could feel the sensation starting to run up my stomach as the pressure increased.

Men learn, perhaps are taught, that any pressure to the balls is painful and hurts. It doesn't. Unlearning such condition can take time. Yes, there is an intensity where pain overrides pleasure, but much of the sensation is actually quite beautiful. Hurrying and surprise give conditioning more opportunity to intervene. A kick in the balls or being hit and the immediate sensation is such that the body wants to respond to 'pain' by bending, to provide protection. More slowly and that broad band of sensation between pleasure and pain becomes so much more difficult to define. The expert can balance a subject on that line for a long time, gradually pushing the point of pain through waves of intensity and then relief.

Mr Woods was doing this.

'A man's being is his balls,' he said quietly. He was both pulling and squeezing mine at the same time. He had pushed the shorts down over my hips out of his way. I leant back trying to give him easier access.

'Yes,' he sighed, 'Oh, yes. There is something so beautiful about having another man's entire being in your hands, especially when he is offering it.'

He pulled harder and squeezed harder.

I could feel my mouth opening and my breathing deepen as the intensity grew. I was sure the picture was beautiful too, but I didn't open my eyes.

'That's nice,' he said, squeezing again.

'Thank you, Sir,' I whispered.

'No, thank you, Jimmy,' he said, pulling more on the sac. There was a sudden tug. Then, without warning, he let go. My body fell forward a little. I fought to catch my breath. I didn't have long. My mouth fell again the Master's cock, hard but still trapped in his own bikini briefs. I had forgotten those.

'Now,' he said, bending forward to his mouth was close to my ear, 'lick.'

My mouth and tongue were dry. I had been breathing hard through my mouth as he had played with my balls. I tried to get my saliva flowing.

I felt Mr Woods 'assume the pose'. He folded his arms across his chest, thrust his groin forward and spread his legs. I went to work. I kissed each ball in the pouch and then the cock head. It was my ritual, but it felt appropriate. Mr Woods hadn't told me not to, or to stop. I felt it had been accepted. I started licking first, trying to dampen the material with my saliva. I licked on ball, then both, then one then both before moving my attention to the erect cock.

I licked it upwards, in tracing strokes, the movement starting in my back, my head moving upwards pulling my tongue after it. I lingered around the cock head, trying to tickle it with my tongue through the material. I tried to find the piss slit. I wondered if anything was starting to ooze out. I hoped so. I left the cock for a moment and licked round to each side. I darted backwards and forward to kiss or lick one or each of the balls, either just glancingly or more intensely for a moment or two. I didn't want the Master to know where the next sensation would be. I kept licking as I shuffled round beside him. I nuzzled my tongue down between his legs from the front as deeply as I could, at last rejoicing in the valley behind his balls. Then, as quickly as I could, I brought my head round behind him.

The Master appreciated my movement. He bent forward and spread his legs a little more. I licked greedily at the material, slowly working backwards. It was too tight to allow me to push right in to lick his hole, but I tried not to let my disappointment become too apparent. Gradually, I slowed my motions and broadened the sweep of my actions. I shuffled again and kissed each cheek. I hoped this felt as respectful as I intended it to be. I could feel the firmness of each round buttock. I wanted to chew them. Instead, I nuzzled them, feeling my mouth pushing against the flesh. I licked each upwards, describing decreasing arcs from close to the hole round in semi- circles to the small of the Master's back. I alternated one side then the other. He appreciated what I was doing. It wasn't until I had completed a full sweep, almost entirely vertical up the divide in between his cheeks and kissed the target that he stepped forward.

I felt a sense of loss for a second. At last I opened my eyes. He was standing with his back to me no more than a foot away. I looked up at the broad shoulders and down the V of his back to the round cheeks. My eyes were at that level when he turned.

I looked up at him. There was, I could see, pleasure in his eyes. I was glad. I was proud. He smiled. He bent forward and gently kissed my forehead. I was in heaven. I looked at this vision in front of me. It was like something from a picture, something I never thought I would experience in real life. The body was strong, but more, the cock and balls in the bikini were like an explicit picture too. I closed my eyes for a second, remembering adolescent masturbation, imagining myself in just the position I was now. I sighed, gasped, smiled and relaxed a little.

I opened my eyes and looked up into his. I'm not sure exactly what it was, but there was something in his expression which told me that he knew exactly what I was thinking. My heart soared. He reached slowly for the draw cord in the briefs and pulled the bow undone. He stepped forward and put his hand behind my head.

'You know what to do,' he said.

I performed my ritual once more. I kissed first the cock head, the left ball, then the right. I bent to kiss behind them and returned to the cockhead. I looked up. The Master smiled. I nodded to express my gratitude, as much as I could with my mouth pressed against the pouch. I ran my tongue behind the waistband. I hadn't had permission, but I tried to see if I could reach to taste his cockhead. I just nuzzled it. He pulled back a fraction, knowing precisely what I was trying to do. I took the material between my teeth. I had to work round him to ease it off his hips. Then, his erection had grown so strong that I had to pull the material back to let his cock escape. I let my cheek brush against it as I pulled the material down to his thighs.

'All the way,' he said, when I paused.

I took the material between my lips and gradually pulled it down. I could smell his perspiration from the run on the lining. It was so dominating my sensations that I almost lost my balance as I bent to pull the briefs past his knees. I had to open my own legs to steady myself. I rested with my chin on the floor when I reached his ankles. He stepped out of the garment.

He let me recover for a moment.

He leant forward and pulled me up. I kept the briefs in my mouth. When I was kneeling upright he took them from my mouth. He held them for a moment. He looked down to my hands. I reached up and took the briefs from him and held them in front of me, in supplication.

'Hold them under your chin,' he said, 'and open your mouth.'

I did as I was told.

Again I looked up at him. It was the first time I had seen him entirely naked. It was a beautiful sight. I looked into his eyes as he placed his cock in my open mouth. I could feel it as he laid it down on my tongue. I could see as he closed his eyes. It was difficult swallowing with my mouth open, but I did it. I felt his erection subside a little. I was inspecting the definition of his pectoral muscles when the first liquid hit the back of my throat. It took me a moment to realize what was happening. I wanted to close my mouth to make swallowing easier, but stopped myself. I started drinking as much and as quickly as I could.

I looked up. The Master's eyes were open again. He smiled. 'Good boy,' he said.

I had to look down again to concentrate on swallowing his piss. It tasted a little salty but that was all. He must have been drinking water for a while before the run, I thought. The flow increased. I could feel some of the piss running out of my mouth and down my chin onto the briefs. My swallowing couldn't keep pace with the flow, they were quickly drenched. Piss dripped down onto the floor between my legs. When the flow stopped, he pushed my face to the floor. I lapped up the piss that had been spilled as thoroughly as I could. When he was satisfied, he pulled me back up. He took the briefs from my hands and wiped my chin with them.

I thought for a moment we had finished. How wrong I was.

'Open your mouth,' he said.

I obeyed. He squeezed the briefs over my tongue so a few more drops of his piss fell into my mouth. I savored them. He then pushed the garment into my mouth. I closed my lips to hold it in place. I hadn't noticed the cord hanging over the shower rail. The Master reached for it and wound it round my head. I opened my mouth to let it pass between my teeth. He wound the rope round twice and tied it behind my head.

'A little something for you to enjoy,' he said, as he stood back.

I looked up into his eyes. I could feel some dampness running out of the sides of my mouth and down my neck. He smiled.

'Peter,' he called.

I stayed kneeling, my hands behind my back. A few moments later there was a knock on the door. The Master opened it. I heard the rattle, but couldn't see anything. I felt the colder body of Peter behind me, helping me to stand. A second later the cuffs were snapped into place behind my back.

'Cleaned and plugged,' the Master said. 'Half an hour.'

I felt in a daze as Peter turned and guided me out of the Master's bathroom.

Preparation

I was glad Peter was there to lead me down the stairs. I was so high. I reveled in the taste of the Master's piss from the briefs that were tied into my mouth. I could feel a trickle of dampness down my throat and across my chest. Yes, I was definitely pleased that someone as experienced, knowledgeable and sensitive as Peter was with me.

'It's okay,' he whispered as we reached the bottom stair. 'Think of this as a continuation, not a break.'

I reached to hold him close to me as we went through the door. He let me relax for a moment, resting my head on his shoulder, feeling his naked skin next to mine and putting a comforting arm around my back. He let me get my breath back.

However, as soon as my chest was moving regularly again, he moved away.

'Stay there,' he said, as he went to the shower cubicle and turned on the water. He turned the tap on the shower head so that the water was coming out of the stainless steel douche nozzle. With his hand in the flow, he waited a moment for the water to reach an appropriate temperature.

Peter let the nozzle fall for a moment, the water quickly draining away. He reached for the cord at the front of my shorts and undid it. He pushed them down my legs determinedly. I stepped out of them.

Then, Peter reached for the pot of lubricant on the stand beside the washbasin and pushed my upper body forward. I followed his wish and bent forward. He scooped up some of the white cream with two fingers and pushed it into my hole.

I gasped. It felt clinical, being prepared by Peter in this way, but good at the same time. At one time, I would have considered this procedure humiliating, especially when it was carried out by another slave. Now, I had moved on. Humiliation was something for others. It was for those who were unable or unwilling to take pride in the service and pleasure they provided for their masters. Kneeling and licking my Master's boots in a bar was no longer a matter of humiliation, it was a display of pride, perhaps even arrogance. It could certainly be showing off, letting the others see that you didn't 'feel bad' about such performances. If anything it was gesturing to them, 'get you, I'm together enough to do this and get off on it'.

Peter smeared the cream into my hole. I could feel him pushing it passed the outer sphincter. He moved me towards the shower cubicle. I stepped in. He turned me round and pushed my upper body forward again.

'Ready?' he asked. He needn't have done. I nodded against the gag.

I felt the water against my hole and then running down the

backs of my legs as Peter brought the nozzle towards me. Then, suddenly, I felt the pressure against my hole as the metal was being pushed, gently, firmly and steadily in. For a second, I felt the water disappear from the back of my legs. Then, the other sensation hit me. I could feel myself being filled. I gasped. I did every time.

Peter slowly pushed more of the metal into me. I could feel as it passed the muscle. He didn't go any further. He held it there. I could feel the water running up into me. I could feel it running down again, the pressure against the muscle building up.

I closed my eyes. The pressure was becoming more intense. Then suddenly, the metal nozzle was gone. I struggled to tighten the muscle, to hold everything in.

'Squat,' Peter ordered.

I did.

'Now,' he said, 'let it go.'

I relaxed. I could feel the water gush out of me. I could feel the muscle opening and closing too. I felt the flow reduce to a trickle. I was glad the smell wasn't too bad. I could feel the water around my feet as Peter used the nozzle to wash what had come out of me down the drain.

'You're fairly clean,' he said dispassionately, 'but we'd better give it another couple of goes, just to make sure.'

I stood again and bent forward. The nozzle entered me again. With my rectum and lower gut emptier, it took longer before the pressure on my sphincter grew. I could feel the warm water being forced upwards through my intestines to my stomach. Looking down, I could see the bloating beginning.

'Squat up and down,' Peter said, 'Ten, starting now.' I moved to do as he said.

Each time I bent my knees, the pressure on my sphincter increased. It became harder with each movement to hold the liquid inside me. I was sure the muscle would fail.

'Stop,' he said as I bent my knees for the tenth time. He made me wait. I had to close my eyes as I concentrated on keeping the muscle tightly closed.

'Okay, let go.'

It was only probably ten or fifteen seconds, but the delay had felt like an hour. I relaxed. The relief was beautiful. Without realizing it, I also started pissing. The water that had been introduced to my rectum was coming out of my bladder.

As before, there was a huge initial gush before the flow died down. Peter let me squat and dribble while he washed the debris away.

'Once more,' he said.

Again I stood.

This time it seemed as if he wasn't putting quite as much liquid into me.

Again, he made me move up and down to make sure that the water cleaned me inside as thoroughly as it could.

Suddenly, as I was waiting, squatting on my haunches for permission to let go, he turned the tap and the shower water hit me from above. I jumped. It felt cold.

'Don't move,' Peter said. 'Yet.'

I stayed where I was. The water got warmer. I had been so entranced from my time with the Master that I hadn't realized that Peter had carefully filled me with water at body temperature. He'd wanted to avoid the internal cramping that could be caused by liquid that was too hot or too cold.

I could feel my hair getting wetter, water running into the side of my mouth round the ropes and the briefs. Of course it felt strange, I thought, I didn't usually shower while being gagged with rope and a pair of Speedos. I enjoyed the warm water running down my back as I waited for Peter's word to let go. It finally came.

I looked down for the first time.

The water running out of me looked clean. I was pleased. If the Master was going to use my ass, I didn't want him to encounter anything unpleasant or unexpected.

Peter pushed me so that I was standing. He handed me a bar of soap. I washed myself down. It didn't take long. I ran the soap between my legs and into the crevice of my ass. I made sure that the sweat from the run was cleared from under my arms. I bent and washed around my ankles and between my toes. I moved carefully so that the water could run over my ballsac and the cockring I was still wearing. I washed carefully between the back of my balls and my hole.

'Done?' Peter asked after a few minutes.

'Yes,' I tried to say, against the gag. A mumbling sound emerged. It could have been 'yes' or 'no'. I nodded too.

That didn't stop Peter. He reached in and turned off the water. I could still have been covered in soap. A moment later, I was handed a large, luxurious towel.

'Dry yourself,' Peter said, 'and then sit on the toilet. Make sure the last of the water is out.'

I ran my hands down my body to push off as much water as I could before I used the towel. It was warm and comforting. I dried carefully around my cock and balls; with the cockring, any moisture left could cause chafing, I thought.

Peter had left the room when I stepped out of the cubicle and lifted the toilet seat and sat down. I wrapped the towel around my shoulders and used the ends to catch water dribbling from the briefs in my mouth.

It took a few moments, but a little more water did dribble out of me.

'Stand,' Peter said, when he came back into the room. He looked into the toilet bowl.

'It's clean. You'll do,' he said, smiling at me.

He pushed me forward before flushing the toilet.

It was then that I noticed the black butt plug beside the basin. Peter saw me looking.

'It's only a medium-sized one,' he said. 'I chose it for you carefully.'

'Thanks,' I thought, sarcastically. I tried to smile against the gag. Peter patted my butt.

'I'll show you the one Morgan takes,' he said. 'That will give you something to aim for.'

I tried to grin. I couldn't.

I hoped I'd be able to take the plug. And keep it in. I'd had one in before, but never for longer than about half an hour, and then it had been played with, put in and taken out, put in and taken out.

'Are you ready?' Peter asked.

I didn't respond. I felt as if I didn't have any choice. I didn't. Again he reached for the pot of white lube. He pulled it towards him. He opened one of the drawers in the unit beside the basin and pulled out a condom. He opened the foil pack and unrolled the latex onto the black rubber plug.

'This way it means we all can use them,' he said.

He must have seen my puzzled expression.

'Don't worry; it's also been in the microwave,' he explained, trying to reassure me.

I choked a little as my attempt at grinning allowed liquid to run back into my throat. I might have known that Peter would have been expert in making sure that the full potential of every domestic appliance had been investigated and applied.

'Bend,' he said. 'Put your hands on the toilet seat.'

I did. Water dripped from my mouth. It didn't seem to worry him. I tried to look back over my shoulder or between my legs to prepare myself, but I couldn't see what Peter was doing. I heard him scoop up some lube from the pot and put it on the plug. I felt the coolness of his fingers as he opened my hole and pushed some lube inside. 'Here it comes,' he said, patting the side of my butt.

My muscle instinctively tightened as the rubber started its invasion. Peter felt it.

'Relax,' he said, 'It's easier that way.' I nodded.

He sighed.

'Don't worry,' he said. 'I'll help.'

He started rubbing the tip of the black rubber plug against my hole, coming in a few millimeters and then out again. The stimulation worked. My muscle responded. It didn't take more than a moment before it was opening of its own accord. Peter pushed the cone shape in and out further. I started to breathe more deeply as the fucking continued. I could feel the flange at the widest part of the plug stretching my sphincter muscle. It wouldn't be very much longer before it was in. My cock responded too, getting thicker, but not fully erect.

Peter noticed that too. No sooner than the plug was fully in for the first time, my muscle contracting over the narrow neck than he said 'push'. I obeyed. My muscle stretched and the plug came out with a 'plop.' Again, Peter said. He pushed the plug in all the way. He let it rest a moment and then, a second time, said 'push'.

I did.

'Here we go,' he said. I relaxed. He put his hand against the flat base of the plug and pushed. It went home easily.

'Now,' Peter said, 'turn round and sit down.'

I did.

My eyebrows nearly crossed my forehead as the tip of the plug hit my prostate.

Peter noticed. He grinned.

'They're never comfortable if you leave them the first time,' he explained. 'You'll be able to go far longer with it now.'

I wondered if that was a good idea. There was no way,

gagged as I was that I could ask how long that would be. Peter looked at the clock on the wall.

'We've got five minutes,' he said. 'I'd better take you up.'

I grinned. I had a better idea of how Morgan probably felt when I'd met him that first time, six days earlier.

Breakfast

It was still dark when Peter shook me awake. I tried to brush him away. It took me a few moments to realize where I was. As soon as I did, I tried to hurry.

Peter held his finger to his lips and then put his hands on my shoulders. It was another moment before I appreciated my predicament. Even if I'd wanted to, I wasn't going anywhere. I was chained to the foot of the Master's bed.

Through my sleepiness and tiredness I tried to remember what had happened. I remembered being taken up to the attic space by Peter. I remember walking awkwardly as the plug settled into my hole.

I remember him coming up later, much later, and finding me in the stocks. He had picked up the used condom from the floor and tidied the space before unlocking my feet. He'd had me step into a cup jock which he had pulled into place before he released my hands. I remember him working some balm into my shoulders. He had brought me a milk drink. It was all I had had to eat or drink that evening. Only then, had he let me come down the ladder.

At that morning moment, I couldn't remember any more. I knelt up. I felt a chain between my hands. Peter was trying to get a key into a lock. As soon as he'd undone the cuffs, I shook my wrists. It felt better to be free, or at least as free as I would ever be in the Master's house, I thought.

'Kitchen, now,' Peter whispered.

It was an effort and required great concentration to stand,

quietly creep across the room and open the door. I dreaded making any noise.

It was only as I reached the bottom of the stairs that I realized just how much I needed to piss.

I went into the closet and lifted the toilet lid. I pulled the cup jock down and let flow. I closed my eyes and felt the relief as the flow of yellow liquid hit the bowl. It didn't take long. I took deep breaths, trying to get as much oxygen into my system as I could. When the piss had finished, I pulled the jock back into place. I ran my hands under the tap and splashed some cold water across my face. I felt more awake. That was better.

I hadn't expected the Master to be outside when I opened the closet door. Peter was standing half a pace behind him. His expression made me fear the worst.

The Master looked me up and down. I suddenly felt shame, and confusion. I bowed my head and put my hands behind my back.

'You shouldn't have done that,' the Master said, 'not without my permission.'

I closed my eyes. I realized what I had done. I hadn't intended to be disobedient or to displease the Master. I'd needed a piss, the first piss of the morning. I shivered. Tears were filling the sides of my eyes.

The Master turned and climbed the stairs.

I was left standing there. It wasn't until we heard the door of his room close that Peter moved towards me. He put his hand on my shoulder and steered me towards the kitchen.

'Now, you know,' he said. 'Slavery isn't just the sexual excitement. It does mean control.'

I nodded.

'Control over the smallest matters, the actions you took for granted, never gave a second thought. You have to learn them all over again. You no longer take those decisions,' Peter said. 'The Master does. You must know to get his permission.'

I knew that I should have known. I had had enough experience. I had read enough. I had known enough others. I closed my eyes and cursed myself. I put my head in my hands when we reached the kitchen.

Peter could see my remorse.

'You'll do it again,' he said.

I looked at him defiantly. Not if I had anything to do with it, I thought.

'I do,' he said, 'even after all this time.'

I looked at him in amazement.

'Yes, of course I do. I become complacent. I stop thinking. I go onto auto-pilot, take things for granted, and what happens? Without appreciating it, I've done something without permission.'

'You do?' I said

'Sure, every so often,' Peter admitted. 'He likes it too.' I looked puzzled.

'He enjoys your punishment, but he won't punish without reason. He is fair,' Peter said.

'Will I be punished for that?'

'Of course,' he said. 'But you won't know when.'

I took a deep breath.

'I'm sorry,; I said. 'I didn't mean it.'

'I know that,' Peter said. 'He knows that too. He knows you're like me, you don't like being disobedient, but he knows too that you're learning, that you're only just starting your transition. He knows that you need some help, some reminders, some incentives.' I stood quietly for a minute. I hoped the punishment wouldn't be too harsh. I would accept it, obediently, quietly. I knew it had to happen. Peter was right about what the Master said. It was necessary to help me on my journey; to help as I examined everything that society had told me about life, about behavior and about roles. Each aspect of my condition would be identified, assessed and only then rejected or replaced.

Peter handed me a mug of coffee. I'd been so engrossed in my thoughts that I hadn't even realized that it was being made.

'I know it's ironic,' he said, 'but be proud. You've just learned another lesson, taken another step.'

I hadn't looked at it that way. I reached for his hand. I squeezed it.

'Thank you,' I said.

Peter let me hold him for a second or two longer.

'We have tasks,' he said. 'First, there is the Master's coffee. You can take it this morning.'

'Are you sure?' I asked, feeling especially vulnerable after the events of the last few minutes.

'He is sure,' Peter said, emphasizing the 'he'.

'Everything's here on the tray. There is a mug, a cafétiere, a jug with some milk. When you go up, knock on the door, put the tray on his dressing table, and finish making the coffee. Then open the curtains, pour the coffee after that and add a little milk. Put the mug on the table beside his bed.'

I was trying hard to remember Peter's instructions.

'Then, fold our bedding. Put it under the foot of his bed. Lay the chains on top of it,' he said.

I nodded.

'Then, not before, kneel at the side of the bed. He will tell you when he wants you to run his bath or turn on the shower.'

Peter saw my look of panic.

'Don't worry. I've put a card in his bathroom telling you what to do, how he likes it.'

I relaxed. 'You ready?'

'As I ever will be,' I said, reaching for the tray. 'I feel as if I'm treading on your territory.'

'Just remember, as I have to, that the territory isn't mine, or yours, or Morgan's, it's his. That's why we're here isn't it?' I felt great admiration for Peter's magnanimity as I picked up the tray and headed for the stairs.

I used the door frame to balance the tray as I knocked on the Master's door.

I had to wait a few moments. It was almost as if he was keeping me waiting on purpose, before I heard the words 'come in'.

Mr Woods was lying in bed reading the paper as I entered. He must have picked it up when he came downstairs, I thought.

I tried to remember Peter's instructions. I put the tray down and pressed down the handle on the cafétiere. I opened the curtains and then returned to pour the coffee. I took the mug to put it beside him. It felt right to kneel as I did so.

He looked over his glasses, taking his eyes off the paper for only a second or so to acknowledge me. I stood and went to clear the bedding.

Peter and I had shared a comforter on a sheet at the foot of his bed. It was where Peter usually slept. I wasn't sure whether it was because I was a newcomer or a visitor that I'd been chained. It wasn't mine to question that anyway, I thought. I picked up the comforter and folded it carefully. I pushed it under the bed. The pillows we were each allowed followed. I then bent carefully to pick up the sheet. The floor had been warm and more comfortable than I had expected. Picking up the sheet, I found out why. Under the thick rug that had acted as our mattress was a thick sheet of foam rubber. I quickly folded the sheet, placed it carefully beside the pillows under the bed and went to kneel at the Master's side.

It was a while before he spoke. 'You know, don't you?' he said.

It took me a moment to realize what he meant. He was referring to my disobedience.

'Yes, Sir, I do,' I said.

'You are not happy with yourself, are you?'

Like Peter, he seemed to know me very well.

'No, Sir, I'm not.'

I looked down at the floor in shame.

Punishment

The punishment when it came was as bad as Peter had said. It started at nine. Peter had taken me round the house. We had collected all the underwear from the Master's laundry basket. It had included the briefs that Peter had been wearing and those that had gagged me the previous evening.

This, I had thought, shouldn't be too bad. It wasn't until Peter took me to the closet and pulled out my own bag that the full implications hit me. I stood at the door as he lifted the items out and put some into a row of buckets. He had been right, it would take me hours. For the first time, I wished I hadn't been such an active collector.

Peter was silent; his expression was enough. You only have yourself to blame, it said. In more ways than one, I thought. When the buckets were full, Peter left. I stood there. He returned a moment later with the Master.

Mr Woods stood between me and the buckets. I could hear as he undid his button fly. He had his back to me so I would be deprived of the sight of his cock. He moved his legs apart. I could see the liquid as it fell towards the first bucket. He stepped sideways without stopping pissing to aim at the second, and the third. The flow stopped. I could see his arm move as he shook the final drips from his cock.

He nodded at Peter.

Peter pushed his briefs down to his thighs. He closed his eyes. It was a few seconds before the piss started to appear. He bent his legs a little to make sure it hit the garments in the bucket. He opened his eyes. Mr Woods nodded and he shuffled awkwardly sideways so that his piss went into the second, and then the third bucket. When the flow came to an end, he bobbed up and down so the drips fell from the piss hole. He waited for Mr Woods' approval before pulling his briefs back into place.

It took me three hours. I carried two buckets, Peter one. In the laundry room at the back of the kitchen, I worked. I thought I'd got the first lot done. I'd left them in a bucket and moved on to the second when Peter came through from the kitchen. He looked carefully into the bucket and shook his head.

I rinsed them twice more, squeezing each item by hand between the two lots of water.

I washed each item by hand, carefully, rinsing them time and again to make sure that all the soap and piss was clear. I wasn't sure whether I should count them all. I wanted to, but I didn't think it would be that good an idea. There were so many, it was probably better not to know. There were some items I didn't immediately recognize. They had been worn either by the Master or by Peter during the week. They might even have been worn by Morgan. I wondered if he was allowed to wear underwear with his metal chastity device. I would have to remember to ask, I thought. Peter would probably know and would tell me.

I did recognize the Speedos that Peter had been wearing the previous weekend. I noted the jockstrap that I had been in when I had arrived for the first time eight days before. The square cut Speedos I'd bought that week were obvious.

As instructed, I had started by soaking every item. Peter had provided me with the bottle of environmentally-friendly washing liquid. I'd let each item soak before starting the rinsing. It was only at that stage that I appreciated the other nuance of the Master's requirement; there was no hot water in the laundry room.

It wasn't long before I really started to feel the coldness in my fingers. The room itself was warm enough. I felt comfortable there wearing no more than a jockstrap. It was my fingers that suffered. I tried clenching my fists between each sink full of water. It helped a little, but not much. I tried holding my fingers under my arms. That made me feel colder all over. I wondered if there was a heater in the room. I looked round. There wasn't anything obvious that I could see. I just held my fingers, and squeezed them with my other hand. That brought a little relief. I stood, relaxed my wrists and shook my hands, trying to encourage the blood flow along my arms. The benefits were short-lived. It tried letting the water run on its own. The garments floated, but it didn't seem to make a lot of difference in rinsing the detergent out of them. I had no option but to plunge my hands into the water yet again. It wasn't actually freezing; it just felt like it.

I shivered.

I tucked my hands between my thighs and squeezed. There was a moment of relief.

Drips of cold water ran down the inside of my legs. I rinsed some more.

Again I tucked my hands between my thighs. More drips ran down my thighs. I shivered.

I rubbed my hands together. I shook them. Progress had slowed. I wanted a break.

I knew Peter was in the kitchen. I also knew that there was no way I should appear until I felt my task was complete. With a determined effort, I could rinse six items before I needed to try to take some of the pain away from my fingers. I appreciated the predicament. My shoulders were warm; my fingers icy. I closed my eyes more and more often as I tried to wish the pain away.

I opened my mouth and let out a silent shriek.

'Ow,' I yelled, mouthing the shape of the sound, but letting no noise past my throat. 'This hurts. Badly'.

Again, I took another deep breath and immersed my hands in the sink full of cold water. I rinsed four, five more items and lifted them on to the draining area before escape became imperative. Another break and then another four, five, six more items; I was making progress. There was no clock in the room. I started counting the time for myself.

I made myself rinse the six items before allowing myself the luxury of warmth for a count of thirty. I moved my hands around as much as I could in that time, trying to encourage my circulation to be as effective as possible. I knew that if I didn't make such a determined effort the task would take longer and the punishment would be greater. Another count of thirty and another six items; I kept going.

Sometimes when I stopped to warm my hands I closed my eyes and put my head back. I tried not to think why I was there. There was no obligation at this stage, I thought. I did not have to be there. I hadn't signed a contract. This hurt, I thought. This wasn't nice. This wasn't sexual. This wasn't a turn on. Why was I doing it? The question kept coming back. Why didn't I turn and leave? Walk passed Peter? Go to the closet, get dressed, pick up my few possessions and leave?

I knew somehow that I couldn't do that. I knew, deep inside me, that I had to do it. Yes, some of it was for the Master. Most of it was for me though. The other painful experience was that I didn't know why. That was hurting too, I thought. I'd thought I'd known myself really quite well. I was learning – the hard way – that perhaps I didn't know myself quite as well as I thought I had. Should I try and find out why I needed to do this, to put myself through such purgatory?

Perhaps that was the lesson? Perhaps I needed the trauma of the distress and discomfort to appreciate the pleasure as it should be appreciated?

'Don't even think about it,' Peter said.

He'd come into the laundry room to check my progress. I'd been so engrossed with my thoughts that I hadn't noticed him.

'Think about what?' I said.

Peter grinned.

'It,' he said, without further explanation. He smiled.

'What did you think I was thinking about?' I said. The question felt clumsy. I was too cold, too pained to think any more about sentence construction.

'About leaving,' Peter answered.

'Actually, I wasn't,' I said.

Peter raised his eyebrows, questioning my honesty.

'I mean it,' I said.

'So what were you thinking about then?' he said.

'You really want to know?'

'Yes,' he said.

'Why I am here,' I answered. 'Why I am doing this. Why I am letting myself be put through this.'

'I think,' Peter said very quietly, 'you already know the answer.'

I screwed up my face and held out my hands.

'I'm not sure,' I said. 'I know I need to be here, have to be here. I don't know why.'

'Then perhaps you shouldn't think about it,' Peter said.

'Perhaps you should just let things happen, go with them, experience them, endure, maybe even enjoy them. Then, later, think about them, examine and explore them. Maybe then, there will be that innermost, that nanosecond of self-discovery that will guide you towards the answer.'

He looked very far away at that moment.

I waited before saying any more.

It wasn't until he focused on me again that I spoke.

'You seem to know a lot about it?' I said.

'You were very eloquent.'

He looked embarrassed.

'It's been on my mind too, you know,' he said. 'I've been there, done it and washed the underwear too.'

I smiled.

'You have to admit,' Peter said. 'It does give you time to think.'

I sighed.

'Yes, Peter, it certainly gives you time to think.'

* * *

There were so many items that the Master came to the laundry room to check them. I had learned my lesson by the time he nodded and I was permitted to fill the tumble dryer. The jock I'd been wearing was damp – with spilled water and perspiration.

'You were lucky,' Peter said, when I finally came back into the kitchen. He could have made you piss on them again. If he does that you have to drink water at the same time.'

I looked at him in amazement.

'It's true, usually at least a pint for each bucket, so you have the piss in you if it's needed.'

I took a deep breath. I was glad that hadn't happened.

'Sometimes he may make you wear handcuffs,' Peter said.

I winced at the thought. I'd thought this morning's endeavors were hard enough. I'd had to divide each bucket up in to several separate smaller loads – jocks, briefs, boxer briefs and Speedos, then whites and colors. I'd washed each and then rinsed them several times. It had taken me ages before the water was clear. I hadn't realized how much dye ran from some of the colored ones. The Master obviously did, as they took rinse after rinse after rinse before the color stopped running, especially in winter when the tap water was at its coldest.

I grimaced at the thought of trying to warm my hands at the same time as wearing cuffs. I closed my eyes. It took me a moment longer to bring my thoughts back together.

'Do I need to ask whenever I need a piss?' I asked Peter.

'Yes,' he said.

'You? Or the Master?'

'The Master if you are in his presence, but you shouldn't really need to go then. You should ask me at other times, at least for the present. He may decide, in due course, that there are set times when you can go, without always having to ask express permission.'

'I see,' I said. 'And washing?'

'The same,' Peter said, 'apart from when you're in the kitchen with me. You wash your hands there whenever you feel you need to.'

'I understand,' I said. 'May I now?'

'You may,' Peter said. 'I'd advise you to start thinking about every second hour, the even hours.' He smiled.

I felt a great sense of relief as I sat down on the toilet in the closet. I made the most of the few seconds rest and peace.

There was a pint glass of water waiting for me when I got back to the kitchen.

'We have to drink at least four each day,' Peter said. 'Or you will soon. You're on two a day for the time being.'

'Why?' I asked.

'The Master allows us a little coffee but only if we make sure we drink enough water. He does too. It's part of the regime.'

I nodded.

I had learned my lesson. I didn't want to experience that again, with or without handcuffs or piss. The Master had made his point.

Ennui

I spent that Saturday evening watching TV with Peter. There was a rug in the front room. We were allowed in the room when the Master wasn't there but with strict provisos – we could only sit on the mat and we had to be wearing no more than our house attire.

I think Peter had recognized my frustration before I did.

We were close together and could feel the warmth from each other's bodies. We were growing to know one another. We had read the paper. We'd had a go at the crossword, but writing the answers down on a separate sheet of paper rather than on the printed grid. That was the Master's prerogative.

'It's like the saying about inspiration and perspiration,' he said as I reached for the TV remote control. The incongruity of watching inane game shows while sitting on a small mat wearing on a jockstrap was starting to get to me. Peter's comment distracted me; I had been about to start an internal debate about the alternative benefits of a book or some music.

It took me a second to pick up on what he'd said. 'Don't you mean boredom and hyperactivity?' I said. 'Whichever,' Peter said. 'You obviously know what I mean.'

I smiled, pleased that we were establishing a rapport. I'd encountered masters only too keen to have households of two or three boys who hadn't appreciated the complexity of the dynamics.

Each time a newcomer was introduced the number of potential interactions was increased significantly. I wasn't sure how to express it mathematically. I knew the general principal. Have two people involved and there was one dynamic. Introduce a third and the dynamics increased to nine. Add a fourth and they became sixteen. It was something like that. You didn't just have to take the relationship between the master and each individual boy or slave into account; you had to recognize the relationships between each of the boys or slaves.

If anything, those were more important. A little more simple arithmetic revealed that the boys and slaves would most probably be spending more time in their own company than with a master; even taking their contracts and rules into account, they had to be able to get on together, to co-exist, or there would be problems. They had to be able to enjoy and appreciate each other's company. The interests – in addition to the focus on the master and the household - had to be complementary. Banning discussions of religion or politics was more easily said than done. An unintentional, even unspoken, reaction to a politician's comment on the radio or TV news could spark painful arguments. It wasn't just a matter of avoiding potential jealousies.

I had been grateful for Peter's warmth and welcome ever since I had appeared for the first time. I had thought that sharing the Master would have been harder for him than it was.

'Just remember you're here,' he said. 'You're in the warm.

You're dressed erotically. You have had exercise. You have been fed and you are waiting for your Master, the focal point in your life.'

I nodded.

'You are so fortunate. I am too,' he said. 'Just think how many people don't have such security.'

I obeyed. I remembered the nights I'd spent in bars and clubs, hunting for the elusive 'Saturday night stud'. How I'd said no to one, two, even three or four, in the hope that the next would be more attractive, more into my scene. I remembered the weekends when sex at three or four in the morning had been such an effort, because I'd been so tired. I remembered the dismay at waking up beside a beauty and realizing that I'd missed my chance. I'd spoilt it and that I'd probably never see him again.

I remembered the quick, anonymous encounters in the back rooms of bars. They had their uses. They were therapeutic; some cock, but no emotion, I thought. Suck or be sucked. Perhaps even sore tits. Rarely, I remembered, a man who really knew what to do when a pair of balls were put into the palm of his hand.

'Appreciate being here,' Peter said. 'Think of the joy of being here; ready to be used, to bring pleasure, when the Master comes in. Isn't that wonderful?'

I must admit I had to agree.

'And pleasure can come to him in so many forms,' Peter said. 'It might be simply from seeing our obedience, in how we're dressed, in how we are staying on our mat. It may be simply from seeing the pleasure in being in his presence, like a pet, but with so much more because of our humanity and our wish to be there.

'Enjoy the unknown too,' he said. 'We don't know what he'll want when he comes in.'

Again, I had to agree.

'Think about it,' Peter said. 'What could he want?'

'Anything,' I said.

'Quite,' said Peter. 'It could be a whiskey and to sit there, in his chair, to listen to some music, or to read, perhaps watch some TV or a movie.'

'He could want to stroke our hair,' I said.

'He could want us to lick his feet,' Peter said. 'To suck his cock, fuck each other, fist each other. Or just stand, motionless, so he can appreciate the visual effect we have, like living statues ....'

I appreciated his dreams.

'We could be all of those things,' I said.

'Or none,' he added.

I nodded.

'That's the joy,' Peter said. 'The fulfilment. Being ready – for anything, for nothing. Are you ready?'

I had to pause before I answered him.

'I'm not sure,' I said. 'Honestly. I want to be.'

'Good,' he said. 'That's important too. Wanting to be.'

'Yes?'

'It's vital,' he said. 'It's what you are committing yourself to, being ready, being available, even when you don't want to be.'

'I think I understand that,' I said.

'There are times, usually for me in the mornings, when I'm not ready to be used, especially if he wants to fuck me. That takes some effort sometimes,' he said.

'I understand.'

'But don't forget, he does try to make it easier for you ... for me ... for us.'

I looked puzzled.

'That's why he keeps us horny, Jimmy. You should know that. It's easier for us when we're horny, when we want it, when our cocks are likely to be half hard all the time and erect within seconds,' Peter said.

'Yes, I certainly do understand that. Keeping going when

I've cum can be horrendous,' I said. 'It's when there are most questions, most doubts.'

Peter nodded.

'Cause and effect,' he said. 'The Master knows. He appreciates the effects, so he eliminates – or at least minimizes – the causes. He tries to take away any doubts, any reservations.'

'That makes it sound so clinical, so scientific,' I said. 'Improvement through analysis, don't you think?'

'Even so,' I said, 'that makes it sound too much like a psychology textbook rather than something to enjoy?'

'It's all conditioning,' Peter said.

'I know,' I said, awkwardly. 'But, well, I don't know, perhaps I just don't want to admit it, that's all.'

'Don't you just follow your cock?'

'I try not to,' I said.

Peter looked surprised.

'I try to follow my cock and my head,' I said. 'If they're not going the same way, there's usually trouble.'

'You have a point,' Peter said. He remained quiet for a while. 'And now?'

I looked at him.

'You need to ask?'

He nodded. 'Just to be sure,' he said.

'I think they're going the same way.'

A grin escaped on to my lips.

'It feels good being here. I hope I'm not in the way.'

It was Peter's turn to look quizzical.

'No,' he said, reaching to pat my thigh. 'I think you're a good boy. I think your head and your cock are going in the right direction. And your heart. I think you have a lot of potential. I hope you will fulfill it.'

'Will you help me?'

Peter looked at me reprovingly.

'Firstly,' he said, more than a little sternly, 'you know you didn't have to ask that question, but I appreciate why you did, and secondly, you already know the answer.'

I smiled. I patted his thigh.

'You know the answer is "yes",' he said, 'all the way round.'

I moved to kiss him. He pushed me away.

'Much,' he said, 'as I appreciate the gesture, I think it's inappropriate, at least here and now.'

He grinned.

'You're a stickler,' I said.

'I'm a survivor, if that's what you mean.'

I smiled. I felt I had found a friend and a soul mate.

I stretched out on the mat and placed my feet firmly on the ground and raising my knees. I clasped my hands behind my head and raised my face forward. I could feel the cockring moving between my legs as I performed that first crunch.

Peter's grin told me the idea hadn't been entirely a good one. He had his tongue between his teeth, mischievously.

'That's six,' I said as he looked directly at me.

'Keep going,' he said, 'and keep counting.'

I got to thirty before he said I could stop. I was just starting to get warm. I relaxed, thinking it was over. I'd closed my eyes. I hadn't seen him watching the clock.

'And again,' he said, catching me unawares.

I responded as quickly as I could; my feet went to the floor, my hands behind my head. I started bending and counting again.

The second time I got to thirty, Peter said stop again. I sat back this time. I followed his eyes to the clock. He was allowing me a minute's rest, only a minute, between sets. I looked at him as the second hand ticked towards the minute.

'Last set,' he said, 'but fifty this time.'

I started the crunches. Peter was smiling by the time I reached thirty. There was the beginning of pride on his face as I reached forty. He reached and gently, briefly, kissed me on the lips when I collapsed back having reached the fifty target. I'd obeyed his order.

'Think how beautiful you will look,' he said. 'Think how much the Master will appreciate you.'

Even with my eyes closed, breathing deeply, I smiled. I turned over. I waited before I opened my eyes and looked at Peter.

His question came from his eyes too. 'You sure?' they asked. I nodded.

'Don't forget I'm supposed to be a masochist,' I said, immediately regretting the fractiousness of the comment, remembering that the hardest, most severe, most knowing tops are usually other slaves.

'Don't worry,' Peter said, 'I won't.'

He was grinning, smirking, his lips pressed tightly together.

'Tens,' I said as I pushed my chest upwards.

'You wait,' Peter said. 'You haven't been in the gym with him yet, have you?'

I shook my head.

The exercise

'I like,' Mr Woods said, 'to make exercise fun.'

I wasn't quite sure what he meant. I wondered if he meant fun for him, fun for me, or fun for both of us. I doubted that. I'm sure that he would have more fun than I would, especially at the start. There was, he had said when I had been standing at his desk in front of him earlier that morning, room for improvement. I was in reasonable shape, he had said, but I needed less body fat and more definition.

I knew what he meant. Even though Brian had brought the

weights when he'd moved into the apartment, I hadn't had the temerity to use them, at least not that first week.

'I think you're going to be coming here regularly, aren't you Jimmy?' he had asked.

I'd nodded. The confirmation that I had a continuing place in his household had made me speechless at first. I was proud, overjoyed even, that I'd been able to please, to perform, well enough to earn such an opportunity.

'Aren't you?' the Master had repeated, after I'd been silent.

'Yes, Sir, please, Sir, if I may, Sir,' I had stammered, excited and still surprised.

'Good.' The Master had smiled too. 'But you are going to have to learn and to work. You're prepared for that, aren't you?'

'Yes, Sir,' I said.

He had turned and looked at the calendar on his desk.

'How often do you exercise?'

I didn't want to answer his question. What was the least incriminating answer I could give I wondered.

'Not often enough, Sir?' I tried.

'I see,' he said. He smiled. I think he appreciated what I was saying. 'That's a thing of the past now, isn't it?' He was looking at me directly. He wasn't wanting to give me orders. He was wanting me to take the decision myself, to say yes I'd do it because I wanted to, because I had the motivation.

'Yes, Sir,' I said, 'That's a thing of the past.'

'Good boy,' he said. 'I like that. You're learning.'

I felt small in his presence, but big in myself.

'Let me see,' he said, almost to himself, I think. 'We – you and I – will have a little fun this morning. Then, when you leave tomorrow, Peter will give you some further instructions.'

'Yes Sir?'

'He'll talk to you this afternoon, find out a little more about what you have been eating, the sorts of foods you buy ....'

'Yes, Sir,' I said.

'And then a regime will be prepared for you. It's for every day. I mean that. And it never ends. It's a commitment,' he said, looking at me directly, again. 'But, then you know that's what you want, what you need?'

'I do, Sir.' I did. I knew I did. I had wanted to for years, but I'd never had sufficient motivation to do it solely for myself. To do it for him, with him, for Peter and with Peter too, were the added incentives I needed. I looked down, embarrassed in some way that he had found so deep a truth about my own inadequacies so easily. He read that too.

'You're not the only one,' Mr Woods said reassuringly. 'There are many who feel the same, who need a little extra encouragement.'

He smiled.

'Feel good, young man, feel positive as you grow, in stature, in definition, in pride,' he said.

For a moment, he sounded as Peter had sounded the night before. For an instant, I was confused. Then, I realized. It wasn't that he sounded like Peter; it was that Peter was sounding like him. Peter had been taken through the same lessons. Perhaps he had heard others before me. No, I thought, it wasn't a 'perhaps'; he would definitely have heard, have worked with, The Master as he took others through similar experiences. Peter had been learning too, I thought.

* * *

The Master looked good in the gym. He was wearing a tight tanktop and square-cut shorts. The shorts had a diagonal gray and white stripe that met as a V; the outline of his cock, balls and round butt were described perfectly, and he knew it. His white socks were spotless; so too where his training shoes.

I'd had to work hard for half an hour to get the mud from the riverbank run off both sets of shoes. I hadn't been allowed socks. My only privilege had been to exchange a metal cockring for a rubber one. My only attire as I'd cleaned the shoes was a jockstrap.

I hadn't appreciated that the Master's home contained a gym either. There were still parts of the property which I hadn't seen. I'd had to ask Peter where it was. He'd told me I would learn, soon enough, and as I needed to. My nature was to be impatient. Containing my curiosity was yet another lesson I was learning. I'd been instructed to start using the rowing machine when I went in. Peter had told me to re-set the counter when I started. I had done. It had felt strange sitting on the plastic seat with a bare ass. It had also felt beautifully erotic, starting to work away, wearing no more than the jock.

I'd been going for about fifteen minutes and was starting to feel the strain when Peter came in. The challenge was more psychological than physical. The conversation with Peter the night before had helped. There wasn't quite the boredom that I had encountered before when using such machines on my own. I had thought about the pleasure for my Master. That helped.

I was sweating properly when the Master came in. He walked to the machine and stood over the front of it. He moved himself so that his crotch was just at the point where I changed direction at the front of each movement. I looked up at him. He looked at me, questioning me with his eyes. I wondered if he knew what I was asking. I was just starting to try and form the appropriate words when he smiled and nodded. I was just starting to pull. As I relaxed forward, ready to begin the next backwards stroke, I did it for the first time: I kissed the bulge in his shorts. I felt myself putting more effort into each pull. I felt myself appreciating the reward of each touch of my lips. I closed my eyes and smiled.

My reverie was destroyed by Peter.

'Ten,' he said, 'nine, eight .... '

I only had a few more kisses to enjoy. I didn't want to lessen the pace, but I didn't want this to end.

'Three,' Peter said, 'two .... one ....'

I made sure I finished by coming forward to replace the handles in their rest at the front of the machine. I kissed the outline of the Master's cock in the shorts, then each of his balls. He patted my head. I hoped I'd done enough.

'Greedy .... 'he said, half-laughing. 'Don't worry, boy, you will get more.'

I was reassured.

'That's just the warm-up,' said Peter.

His attire – the usual Speedos –seemed an appropriate half-way statement between my jockstrap and the Master's tanktop and shorts.

'Come over here,' he said.

I obeyed.

I was weighed. I was measured, Peter carefully filling in spaces on a piece of paper. He didn't tell me any of the figures. I couldn't see as they were written down. It was yet another time which felt clinical, not erotic.

The bench presses were next. The Master had selected weights which he thought would be appropriate for me. He nodded for me to lie on the bench. I sat, turned and pressed my back down. I made sure my feet were placed firmly and then looked up to grasp the bar. The view was wonderful. I caught my breath. The Master was standing over me, spotting, ready to catch the bar if anything should happen. The space between his legs and the protruding bulge of his balls were my natural point of focus.

'Something for you to aim for, boy,' he said, leaning forward so I could see his face.

'Thank you, Sir,' I said.

He was right. It was a great incentive.

It worked too. I don't think I would ever have managed the three sets of 10 on my own. I'd probably have done the first okay, but then reached eight the second time and six the third. It had taken great effort, but I'd done it. He'd helped too, of course.

When I'd reached eight in the second set, he bent slightly and put one hand under the bar. He couldn't really have been taking any of the weight; it just felt as if he had. He did the same at the crucial sixth repetition in the third set. He had stared directly in my eyes, challenging me to fail, challenging me to let him down.

I hadn't.

I could feel the effort in my arms when the weights finally settled in their rests.

'From arms to abs,' he said, guiding me towards the floor mat.

I got into position. Mr Woods stood over me. He placed one foot on each side of my chest and then lowered himself. The stance must have been good exercise for his own thighs. He knew what he was doing. The first time I brought my head forward in the crunch, my lips met his cock. I didn't take any notice of the numbers that Peter called out. Mr Woods put his hand out to stop me. I waited. When he let go, I started again. I didn't care how much time Peter was allowing me to recover. It was difficult not to dribble. The exertion was making my mouth water. I was sure there was a ring of dampness on the front of the Master's shorts when I was finally pushed back for the last time. I didn't have time to check before I was turned over. I was able to lie still for a few moments. The Master was looking at the figures that Peter had written down. I put my hands and arms in front of me while I tried to catch my breath.

'Push-ups next,' Peter said.

I grimaced. These were my worst exercises of all. I hoped the Master would help again. It didn't take long to find out.

He stepped over me. It wasn't easy to look up but I quickly became aware of his trainers in front of my face.

'There you are, young man,' he said, 'I'm here to help again. Kiss the left the first time, the right the second. Is that clear?'

'Yes, Sir,' I said.

I tried to ignore thoughts of Peter's numbers. It was easier that way, I felt. I just kept going until the Master pulled a foot away. I think I did three sets of twenty. I just knew that I could feel it. I could also feel my cock growing in my jockstrap.

The Master pulled me into a kneeling position when I had finished. He rubbed my head. That felt good. I felt good.

'Squats, Peter?' he asked.

I wasn't sure why the Master had asked the question. Perhaps it was to check their place in the workout. I soon found out.

'Show him how to get ready.'

The Master's voice had changed from a question to an order. I turned.

Peter was pulling an incline bench into the centre of the gym. There was plenty of space around it. He put down his notes and walked across to a cupboard. He came back with what, to me, looked like a pot of lubricant in one hand and some condoms in the other. I remembered the Master saying that he wanted to make exercise fun. I hadn't realized that he was intending to make it so overtly sexual too.

Peter moved to get two dumbbells. One was put on each

side of the bench. He motioned that I should approach. I did. He nodded twice, indicating that I should put a hand on each side of the bench. Again, I obeyed his orders and bent forward.

He didn't touch my jock as he took a scoop of lube and gently inserted two fingers into my hole. The reason for morning douches at the same time as morning showers suddenly became apparent. I could feel the Master walking slowly round behind me, watching closely as Peter performed his task.

Despite the privacy of the Master's home gym, and being accustomed to being nearly naked and being used sexually by the Master, I could still feel my face going red.

'Enough.' The Master had spoken.

Peter pulled his hand away. He wiped the excess lube onto his own thigh. I stayed where I was. I could feel Peter, now formally obedient, standing to one side. Even though I couldn't see it, I could feel the Master's eyes looking backwards and forwards, from one of us to the other.

'Peter,' he said a moment later, 'my shorts.'

I could hear Peter kneel. I could imagine as he bent forward to take the waistband in his mouth. I could hear the slight sound as he pulled the elastic forward over the Master's cock and down his thighs. I hear the slight movement as the Master stepped out of the garment when it reached the floor.

I felt Peter's hands around my waist, pulling me back, upwards and away from the bench. I stood back, my hands clasped behind me, as the Master turned and sat on the bench, his butt at the lower end. He leaned back. His cock was almost hard. I could see as he looked for Peter.

'Get me hard and then the condom,' he said as he put his head back and relaxed.

Peter placed himself between the Master's legs and knelt. He didn't look at me as he did so. I think he didn't feel he had to. I saw he had a condom in his hand, but Peter wasn't going to rush his work. He started gently, licking up the Master's thighs to the inside of his legs. He would gently brush the hair on the Master's balls, but made no definite, determined, effort to touch them. I watched his technique carefully. I was sure I could learn from it.

Peter gradually worked himself up the Master's legs. There was finally a time when he both very gently but firmly pounced on the ballsac. In one graceful, purposeful gesture, his open mouth scooped the balls up from below, he sucked hard and both disappeared into his mouth. It must have taken practice, effort and determination. The Master's balls were not small. They must have been pressing against Peter's throat, I thought. I could see Peter's mouth moving, working hard, licking, chewing, squeezing the Master's ballsac, gently but firmly pulling back on it. The effect was quickly evident. The Master's chest heaved more deeply. I could see the smile of pleasure starting its journey across his face. His cock thickened and jerked. Peter had his eyes closed, his mouth busy and his attention fully occupied.

I was watching in awe, focusing on the Master's heaving abdominal muscles. It was a moment before I noticed Peter's hand waving beside his thighs. He was motioning for me to take the condom from him. I moved forward and did so. He opened his eyes. He looked directly at the Master's cock. My gaze followed his. He nodded. I pulled the wrapping open and, as carefully as I could, pulled out the latex sheath. I placed it on top of the Master's cock. Mr Woods kept his eyes closed as I slowly unrolled the condom along the length of his erection. Peter didn't stop his work on the Master's balls for an instant.

'Jimmy,' the Master said, his eyes still closed.

'Yes, Sir?'

'You know what you have to do?'

'I think so, Sir,' I said.

'Good boy. Place yourself over me, then bend and pick up a weight in each hand.'

'Yes, Sir,' I answered, quietly but firmly.

Peter's eyes indicated that I should stand at the top of the bench, beyond the Master's head and then gradually step backwards until I was in the right position.

It felt awkward. I felt my own jockstrap was too close to the Master's face as I edged back. I had to spread my legs really wide to pass his broad shoulders. I brushed the sides of his chest. I had to be careful to avoid the Master's hands, lying beside him on the floor.

I realized I was in the correct position when I felt the stubble of Peter's head hit my butt. I hoped I hadn't left lube on his forehead. There was no way I could pick up both weights at the same time, I realized. I had to bend first one way, then the other. They were heavy.

I wondered how long I would be able to keep going.

Peter's hands had come round from behind his back. He was resting his chest either on the Master's thighs or on the end of the bench, I thought. I could feel the gentle double tap on my butt. I started to bend my knees for the first time.

Peter must have been holding the Master's cock, aiming it directly at my hole. I could feel it almost as soon as I started moving. I tried to make my descent as smooth and sensuous as I could. I tried to shift the focus of my attention from the weights I held in my hands to my sphincter.

I tried gently squeezing as the Master's cock gradually entered me. I could feel the head inside. I could feel the tip pushing open the inner ring. I could feel my mouth opening. This surely was an effective way to get fucked, I thought. I could feel more of the Master's cock entering me, more easily and more fully than I had ever experienced in any other position before. Only dildos had been so effective.

I could feel myself pushing Peter's head away as I took more of the Master's cock inside me. I was trying to decide whether he was holding onto the ballsac with his lips, pulling gently but firmly, as long as he could. Why was I wondering? He would be I was certain. I closed my eyes as the Master's cock filled me. I could feel his pubic hair against my ball sac. I wondered if I could sit on him. No, I thought, just shaking my head. That wasn't the idea. I could take all of him, but I had to bear my own weight. I had to let my thighs take the strain. I let the cock fill me as fully as possible for a while. My upward motion was as gentle as I hoped the downward movement had been.

The weights in my hands were almost forgotten as I concentrated on keeping my movement as slow as possible. I could feel the strain in my thighs. I came up as far as the head before moving back down again. This time, the motion was a little quicker. My eyes were still closed.

I was still concentrating on keeping the movement steady and gentle when Peter touched my cheek. I hadn't noticed him move. I opened my eyes. He held up all his fingers and then three. I smiled. I was into sets and reps again; three sets of ten repetitions. Peter was standing in front of me. There were barbells in his hands too. He started to bend. I followed.

It was harder work concentrating than holding on to the weights I thought. Peter's movements were very deliberate. Sometimes, I wasn't counting, so I didn't know when, he would stop for a moment, perhaps two or three, on the way down or on the way up. I could feel the Master's cock beautifully within me. I felt him tense too, occasionally, when Peter and I were motionless.

It was hard for me too not to close my eyes. The sensations were so wonderful that sight was superfluous. I wanted to shut it out, to feel, yes, to feel, what was happening to my muscles. Peter let me relax for a while during the last set, to experience the Master's cock deep within me at the bottom of each squat. He would only start to come up again when I opened my eyes.

I hadn't noticed that we had reached the last rep. I was at that lowest point, my legs spread widest, the cock deepest within me when I started to realize that it was swelling inside me even more. I could feel the tension in his abdomen beneath me, in his thighs. I could feel the pulsing grow. Then, like a volcano, his cum was erupting into the latex reservoir deep within me. For a moment, I lamented the rubber, wondering just how up me far his semen would have gone without it, whether I would have felt the ejaculation deep in both my body and soul.

There were tears in my shut eyes when I felt the double tap on my side. I looked down. There was joy in my Master's eyes. A glance to each side told me I should put down the weights. I could feel his cock still hard inside me as I reached down, left first, then right, to put the dumbbells down. I suddenly felt the tension leave my shoulders. My Master was bending up towards me. There was a gentle, beckoning gesture in both hands. I bent forward. I closed my eyes. His lips met mine.

The touch did not last long, a fraction of a second. It was beautiful. It caught me by surprise. I could feel his cock still there, inside me. He was still hard. I was impressed. It took me a moment to realize what was happening. That cock had become so much part of me so quickly that I had forgotten about myself. I couldn't tell whether my cock was hard or soft within my jock. I could only tell that my muscles were tightening. I could feel the tension as my legs fought to straighten, in my sides; I could feel my shoulders pulling back, my arms going behind my back.

I bucked as the liquid shot out of my cock and into the pouch of the jock. I could feel the Master's cock still as I reacted. I could see Peter's expression of horror and astonishment. I looked down. I could see my Master's smile of beauty. The spasm seemed to go on and on. I couldn't help it. I screamed. My eyes were open. Closed. My lips gaping then being licked. The orgasm was a flight. I don't know how long it lasted, the 'oh yes' ran into the 'wow'. My shoulders collapsed. The energy ran down me. So too did the tears.

I could see the dampness spreading out through the cotton of the jockstrap. I could feel the cum start to dribble round my balls. I hoped it wouldn't fall out onto my Master's tanktop, at least not without permission. I tensed again, nervously.

'Relax, boy', he said, very gently as I slowly stopped moving. His cock was still hard in my hole. I was sitting back, a little more easily. My thighs felt as if they had been stretched for ever.

I tried to breathe deeply. It took time to happen. Still, the cock was hard inside me. I could feel my own subside, saturated inside the pouch.

He let me recover. The Master held me while my strength gradually returned. It wasn't easy. Every time I thought I was regaining control over my own body, I felt the cock inside me.

'There's no hurry,' he said, looking directly into my eyes.

I felt reassured. I felt awkward. He was trapped. He noticed my anxiety.

'I said,' he said, looking at me firmly, 'there is no hurry.' He gently raised his hips so I could feel his cock in me, yet again. 'And I mean it.'

I smiled.

'Yes, Sir,' I said. 'Thank you, Sir.'

It took a while, but it was my turn to bend. He responded. He lifted his head to meet mine. I kissed him, straight, directly on the lips.

It was as gentle and quick a gesture as I could achieve.

'Thank you, Sir,' I whispered as my mouth passed his ear.

He tapped me twice again. It was the signal that the exercise was over.

Finally, I moved forward. I rose steadily. I let his cock out of me carefully. I had to close my eyes again to concentrate. There was still some hardness left in it. He let me move forward, stepping past his shoulders before he moved.

I heard him stand. I heard him remove the condom. I heard him start to leave.

I opened my eyes when he stopped.

He turned and came back to me. I could see Peter to one side, the used condom in his hand.

'I think you will do well, Jimmy,' he said. 'You please me.'

A role in life

'That was impressive,' Peter said as he put his arm around me. 'Very impressive.'

'I didn't do it on purpose. It just happened.'

'I know,' Peter said, 'but it was beautiful, very beautiful.'

'You mean that?'

'Of course. So too did the Master. He was pleased, but then you know that already.'

'It's still good to hear it again.'

'We'd better tidy the place up. You'd better shower again and change that jock.'

'There's something I think I should do,' I said.

Peter looked at me, curiously.

'May I?' I asked as I put my hand in the waistband of the jock.

'I don't see why not,' Peter said.

I pushed the jock down and stepped out of it. The cum was still all over the inside of the pouch. I brought it to my lips and started licking. It tasted sharp and salty. I sucked too.

I could see Peter. He was grinning. He caught me eye.

'A good idea,' he said as he reached to put the weights back on a rack. I was still licking the jock as he returned the lube and unused condoms to the cupboard. Peter knelt and picked up the Master's shorts with his mouth. He looked round and then nodded.

We made our way from the gym to the closet. I was still sucking my own ejaculate from the pouch of the jockstrap I'd been wearing; Peter kept the Master's shorts tightly between his teeth.

We washed each other in the shower. We were allowed to do this, Peter had explained, and we could touch the other's cock and balls, but only briefly and to wash them. We could rub against one another, but only use our hands to wash each other.

I just wanted to be with someone, to be close to that person, to put my head on a shoulder, to be caressed. I wanted to be valued and appreciated. I could still feel the effects of my orgasm.

'I've never ever come like that before,' I said to Peter, suddenly, as the water was running down us. 'It usually takes quite a lot of effort.'

He kissed my chest briefly.

'Something was right,' he said. 'Everything was right.'

We were interrupted by the sound of the bell. Peter rushed out of the shower. He grabbed a towel and was drying himself as he ran up the stairs.

He was still dripping when he reappeared at the closet door.

'He wants you.'

I stopped drying myself and put the towel down.

The door to the Master's study was open when I got there. I knelt. It was the custom if the door to a room being used by the Master was open.

'Yes,' he said, a few moments later.

I stood and walked to the front of his desk. I bowed and put my hands behind my back.

It was hard not to cry. Somehow, in that instant, the few moments from kneeling at the door, to standing, a supplicant there in front of the desk so much felt so right. Nothing else in my life mattered.

The Master waited. He let me experience that time. I couldn't say whether I endured it or enjoyed it. I felt a peace with the world. It was a while before I realized that I was naked apart from a metal cockring; that I hadn't replaced a jock or anything after the shower. The Master was dressed, I could see, in chinos, a shirt and tie. He filled the shirt well. At any other time, in any other situation, the differences between us would have embarrassed me. Instead, they felt entirely appropriate.

'You know you didn't have permission?' he said.

'Yes, Sir, I do know that, Sir, but there was nothing I could do about it, Sir,' I added quickly.

'I was talking about permission, young man, not excuses.'

I felt my face redden. I could also feel my cock starting to harden. The jocks or Speedos lessened the embarrassment of that happening, I realized.

'So, what are we going to do about it?'

I looked blank. I hoped I wasn't going to be punished. Not again. I'd learned that lesson already.

The Master looked at me over the top of his glasses.

'Is it going to happen again?'

'I don't know Sir,' I said. 'I hope it does,' he said.

My astonishment must have been very obvious. I felt my mouth dropping open.

'It was spontaneous, boy, and better for it. Your body was telling me what your mouth and your mind would not, perhaps could not. You understand that?'

'I do, Sir, yes,' I said.

'Your body has told you what you wanted to know, hasn't it? That you have found a role in life that is right for you.'

I rested. I knew the Master was correct. At that very moment, I was experiencing something very new to me. I was experiencing fulfillment. I felt valued. I felt appreciated. I wasn't sure that I felt love, but I knew that I felt that I belonged. This household felt right to me. The Master wasn't having to try too much. He knew what he wanted and was comfortable and confident in that.

It wasn't so long before that when I'd come across a guy who presented himself as a master, but he wasn't. He was too disorganized in himself. He was overweight, knew it, wanted to shed some pounds, but didn't have the self-determination or the self-discipline to do it. On the same business trip, I'd met another man, some thirty years younger who oozed his role as Master. He had been a boy. He exercised immense self-control. I hadn't really had much respect for the first guy. He'd claimed to be an experience top too, but when we'd played, he'd gone too far too fast. He'd scared me. I'd turned off. The encounter hadn't worked. I didn't even see the second guy naked. But I knew that when I was in his presence, I shouldn't use the furniture. My slave conditioning came out. I walked two steps behind him when we went out to brunch and to a grocery store. I opened the car door for him.

The Master I was with now was very like the second of those two guys. The first had almost been trying too hard. This man appreciated that I was trying to give. He knew how to accept my offerings, without embarrassment and genuinely. He could cope with the possible scrutiny of the neighbors as we came back from the run, probably even ignore it, confident and strong in his role as head of the household. He was happy taking decisions for Peter and me. He was pleased taking Morgan's gift of his chastity.

I suddenly felt very much older than my twenty-two years. The Master was sitting there, at his desk, watching as I stood silently, immersed in my thoughts. I felt as if I knew far more about what I wanted, needed, from life than so many of my contemporaries. I felt old. I felt lucky too. There was something else. It took me a while to clarify it, to appreciate that it was that there were simply so many emotions. They were happening at the same time, alternatively, repeatedly, with one another, against one another. Yet, despite the parameters on my behavior which I had agreed, that I was developing and agreeing with the Master, I was free to experience all those emotions, in the myriad complexity of their quality and quantity.

'I don't think I really need to say anything, do I?' Mr Woods said, again looking at me over his glasses.

I didn't know what to say.

'I know it may be a little unorthodox, especially to some, but I'll tell you something, Jimmy, young man.'

'Yes, Sir,' I said, curious now.

'I regard what we are doing as a partnership. There are some things you need in your life, some I need in mine. If they are diametrically opposed, equal and opposite, if you will, then we can both grow, develop and find fulfillment, can't we?'

I nodded.

'I'm a little older than you. I've lived more of life and experienced more, so I hope there are some things you can learn from me,' he said modestly.

'You have been here only a short time, but you have shown great promise. You have clearly learned much, even though you are young. You said you had started young. I like that. I am going to test you, but then you know that. It's not going to be easy, but one person's ease is another's pleasure and someone else's challenge. It's up to you to define the experiences as you wish.'

Again I nodded. This man was saying so much that mirrored how I felt. To me, it was common sense. It was joyous to hear it said so clearly and so honestly.

'You are here until tomorrow morning?'

'Yes, Sir.'

He smiled.

I waited as he reached into one of the drawers of the desk. The lecture was over.

'Come here,' he said.

I moved round the desk to get closer to him.

I stood there quietly, my hands still behind my back as he locked the cockring into place. My cock was hard when he had finished, my balls tense against the metal. He slapped my cock. It wasn't a hard slap, but enough to make me start. He looked up and me and smiled.

'Yes?' he said, slowly.

I knew I shouldn't respond.

He turned and pulled some papers towards him.

'Now, take that thing and go and put it away,' he said, 'just in case it's needed later.'

It felt strange, my erection bobbing in front of me as I went back downstairs to the kitchen. I felt like trying to cover myself in front of Peter.

'You'll get used to it,' he said, almost dismissively as he handed me the briefs. I sincerely hoped I would.

Encouragement

Peter had the lists ready for me. We went through them on the Sunday evening. There was a diet sheet, an exercise regime and my clothing instructions.

'You're moving very quickly,' he said as we sat down on the bean bag in the kitchen. 'I've only once known the Master take such trouble so soon after meeting someone.' He looked at me carefully.

'You'd better make sure that his efforts aren't wasted.'

I nodded. I appreciated the trouble the Master was taking. I also felt proud that he considered me worth the investment. I didn't want to let him down.

The diet sheet made me gasp. All fat, well, as much fat as possible, was to be eliminated from what I was to eat. I shouldn't try and buy any, Peter explained. I should keep off cookies, cakes, chocolate bars, chips, and as many snacks as possible. If they weren't too heavy on the fat, they were probably far too heavy on salt, he said. He told me about protein, about beans and pulses and soya. He told me about carbohydrates, about rice, bread, potatoes and pasta. He told me about fruit. I tried hard to remember.

'If you don't buy it,' Peter said, 'you can't eat it.'

It was sensible advice. It was now up to me, I thought.

'Just remember, though,' he said, 'You can eat as much as you want, but if a calorie goes in, it has to be burned off. Calories in calories out. Go have the high-fat calories, by all means, but remember that an hour on a rowing machine in the gym may only burn off seven hundred. You make the calculations, Jimmy, you take the decisions. The discipline, at least when you're away from here, is yours and yours alone.'

I felt daunted by it. Starvation, I felt for a moment, would be easier.

'Make sure you have enough to drink too,' Peter said. 'Two

or three pints of water, nothing with caffeine, every day, and four pints when you're here. That's very important.'

The exercise schedule didn't seem unreasonable in comparison. Peter explained there were exercises I could do at work, on my way to work, from work. There was only one form of exercise which was forbidden, completely and utterly – playing with myself.

'Every time you move a muscle, you're body is using energy, so keeping moving uses calories. Walk, even if it's only up and down as you wait for a train,' Peter said. 'Lift yourself up on tip toe and back down again. You can do lots of sets of those while waiting for buses.'

I looked at him.

'Sure,' he said. 'Okay, there are some things which may get you strange looks, but it depends where you are. I was told about one guy who walked to work through Manhattan raising small weights up and down in front of him as he went. You might attract unwanted attention doing that in London, but you can still keep your body moving.'

'There's plenty to think about,' I said.

'You're coming back Friday?'

'I hope so,' I said, 'If I may.'

'I think the Master will let you,' Peter said, grinning. 'In which case, here's your clothing list. I will put the items out for you in the morning. Don't forget you must bring them all back with you on Friday.'

I nodded and started to read. The choice was straightforward. I would wear Speedos under my work clothes tomorrow and in the apartment when I got home. I'd be in a cup jock in bed. Tuesday was a boxer brief, with the Speedos in the evening.

Wednesday was a test, I saw. I would wear one thong in the morning and another in the afternoon. I would take the second with me and change as close to 1 pm as work allowed. I was to call before two, to say that I had done as I was told. The cup jock which I put on that night, Wednesday, would then stay on until I arrived here again the following Friday.

'That seems okay,' I said, looking up at Peter.

'Have you done anything like this before?' he asked.

'No,' I said.

He smiled.

* * *

I'd been up promptly on the Monday morning. I had to leave the Master's house at seven to be in work on time. My mental alarm had gone off at six. I'd crept out from under the comforter, trying hard not to wake Peter. I tiptoed out of the room, trying to avoid any sounds which might have disturbed the Master.

I showered and shaved quickly, while the coffee was brewing. I put out the Master's mug while my hair dried. I grabbed some bran cereal and skimmed milk while I waited. They were on the list of foods I was allowed, I remembered. The shirt I had worn to work on Friday had been washed and ironed. I put it ready.

I poured the coffee when I heard Peter coming down the stairs. I followed him back up.

I stood formally, just inside the bedroom door as Peter pulled the drapes and put the Master's coffee down beside him. I watched as he went into the Master's dressing room and returned with a small parcel. There was a striped Speedo on the top.

'You have your lists?' The Master said, turning to me.

'Yes, Sir,' I said, 'Peter went through them with me last night.'

'Good. Come here.'

Peter handed the Master some keys. I hadn't noticed them in his hand. He reached for my cockring and unlocked it. Peter handed me a rubber replacement and nodded that I should put it on. With my cock starting to harden, it took longer than I would have wished. The Master reached for the parcel. He lifted the Speedos from the top. He pushed the bedding down away from him and held them for a moment against his own cock and balls. He smiled as he handed them to me. I appreciated the gesture.

I stood for a moment with them in my hands. He nodded. I bent to put them on. They were tight. I could feel my cock held hard against me and the pressure on my balls.

'Let me see,' the Master said. I put my hands behind my back so the obscene bulge could be inspected. He cupped my balls, and then squeezed them, gently at first then more intensely. I could feel the pressure at the sides of my stomach and was having to make a determined effort not to bend forward by the time he let go. He slapped my cock backwards and forwards in its wrapping.

'Turn.'

I obeyed.

The Master tried to run a finger under the elastic seems. It took some effort, they were so tight. He slapped the cheeks of my ass.

'I approve,' he said at last. 'Turn.'

I was facing him again. He took the parcel and gave it to me. I nodded. It seemed the right way to say thank you. 'Friday, six thirty?'

'Yes Sir,' I said.

'Good. Go.'

I turned and went down the stairs carrying the parcel. I went into the closet and dressed as quickly as I could. The

Speedos felt very tight. I made sure my tie was knotted neatly. I'd cleaned my shoes the evening before. I wanted to be smart for my Master as I left the house.

Peter was at the closet door when I picked up my small bag, ready to go. He was holding my wallet. I'd almost forgotten that; he had taken it from me on the Friday evening. It had all my money, apartment keys, and plastic cards in it. The only way I could have left the Master's house over the weekend would have been in shorts, walking and penniless. I had forgotten that. I smiled. Peter grinned. There was no need for words.

'You look good,' he said, before leaning forward to kiss my lips quickly.

'So do you,' I said. His appearance in Speedos matching mine reminded me of the erection trapped inside my chinos.

'Remember,' he said. 'Until Friday, it's all up to you.'

He closed the front door behind me. I wanted to look back, to run back, to be there. I didn't want this world.

The journey to work seemed to last forever. The men who had looked so wonderful just days before seemed dull and gray. I felt lonely, alone. I could feel the tightness of the Speedos. I wanted to strip. I wanted to shed the pretence. I wanted to be me, but the world wouldn't allow it.

I must have walked from the station to the office in a dream. I don't remember it at all. I can recall trying to keep the tears from my eyes. I didn't keep pictures, but I wanted one, of Mr Woods, of Peter. Morgan's appearance in the metal belt appeared in my mind's eye too. That picture was also so beautiful, in its own distinct, erotic way; the metal plate in front of his groin, a shaven ball pushed out to each side. David, my boss, had pictures of his wife and children on his desk; I wanted Mr Woods and Peter on mine. They were my family now, I thought.

I threw myself into work again that day. Activity was a distraction. I filed. I tidied. I cleaned my typewriter. I took two boxes of files to the library for the company archive. I hardly sat down.

Brian brought me down to earth when I got back to the apartment.

'You're in love,' he said. I'd started undoing my chinos as I was shutting the front door behind me.

'Perhaps, I am,' I said. I wasn't sure. Did I love the person? Or the context? Brian's words sounded as if he was accusing me of being in love with a person. Mr Woods was a sexy man, physically and psychologically, but was I in love? I didn't know. Brian's words had found a vulnerability. They'd come at a key moment. I was tired. I was elated. I was trying to think. I felt like a child, wanting its parent. I wanted to cry.

Brian noticed. He came to hold me. He took the chinos from my hands. I must have looked a sight. My shoes were pushed to one side. I was standing in the Speedos, my tie half undone and my shirt tails flapping. My bag lay inside the door where I'd dropped it.

'You're in love with something,' he said.

'But I don't know what,' I said.

He looked at me knowingly.

'You've found something,' he said. 'That shows. It's something very, very important.'

I reached for the bag. I pulled the sheets of paper from the pocket at the side. I gave them to Brian in silence.

I didn't feel I could watch him read them though. That was too personal, too intimate. I picked up my bag and the shoes and took the chinos from him.

In my room, I tried to pull myself together. I hung the chinos on a hanger. I took a brush and dusted off the shoes before putting them away. I took off my tie and put it with the others, hanging on a rail behind the door. I took off my shirt, undid all the buttons and put it into the laundry basket. I caught sight of myself in a mirror. The Speedos looked obscene, but beautiful. I could see the outline of my cock, pointing upwards, held close against my belly. I could see the outline of each ball. I turned. I could see the material framing the curves of my butt. It felt good.

I sat down on the bed and pulled on my boots. I pulled on a sweatshirt. I opened my bag.

The parcel was there, untouched, unopened. I carefully undid the wrapping. There, on top of each other were the garments for the week. There was a white boxer brief, another pair of Speedos, a jockstrap and two thongs. I laid them on the top of my chest of drawers.

I felt I needed to see them, to know they were there, that these apparently small decisions had been taken for me. I bent forward and kissed them.

Brian was sitting at the kitchen table when I walked in. He had the sheets laid out in front of him. I hadn't noticed until then, but he too was wearing a light blue office shirt and cream chinos.

He looked at me for a few seconds before speaking.

'It's good,' he said, 'very good.'

'Thanks.' It was all I could think of saying. I wanted to sit, but it seemed wrong to use the furniture. I didn't feel I could kneel in front of Brian. I sank to the floor.

'You're really into this aren't you?'

I nodded. It was more than 'being into' though. Such words demeaned the fulfillment I was finding. I wondered if Brian really understood. He leant forward and rubbed his hand through the stubble on my head.

I smiled and kissed his hand as it rubbed my cheek.

'Thank you', I said, 'for being there, for understanding.' He smiled.

He lifted his leg. It seemed perfectly natural for me to start undoing the laces of his shoes. I eased the sides apart and held first the right and then the left as he stepped out of them. I put them down neatly, carefully to one side.

I looked up. He was undoing his tie. He undid the top button of his shirt and then tidily folded the tie and put it on the table. He undid each button of his shirt before taking it off. It was only then that he started to undo the fly of his chinos.

I watched, fascinated. Brian had a good body. It was firm and well-defined. I felt my eyes widening as he pulled the chinos apart to push them over his hips. He was not only wearing Speedos, but the same style as me. My eyes must have shown my disbelief. A co-incidence? That was too much, I thought.

Brian turned and pulled the chinos off. The cheeks of his butt were also framed by the tight material. I wanted to lean forward and kiss them. He saw me starting to move forward. He smiled and moved away. I hardly noticed the movement as he shook his head. It was only after he'd folded the chinos and put them on the table that he reached for my hand. He was pulling me to stand. I was opening my mouth, words starting to form. He put his first finger to my lips. It was clear I should remain silent. He led me to his room. I stood motionless. I knew there were some photographs in frames on his chest of drawers. I'd never seen them though. They were behind me now. I felt awkward. I wasn't sure what role I was supposed to be performing. Did roommates behave like this? I didn't think so; there was something far more intimate happening between us. Brian had known some of what was happening. We'd enjoyed the time the previous week. He'd worn the new Speedos I'd bought. But how had he known what I would be wearing today?

I had been gazing into infinity while I thought.

I felt Brian pushing a photograph in a frame into my hands. I looked at it.

I gasped.

There were two figures in the picture. One was standing, wearing a black leather cap, leather jacket, gloves, boots, and chaps over denim. There was a chain in his hands. He was almost stereotypically a master. Beside him, a young man was kneeling, upright, but head bowed. He was wearing only a leather jockstrap. There were rings in his nipples; a fine chain linked them together. There was a heavy metal collar round his neck. There were cuffs around his wrists with a chain between them. A chain ran up between the man's legs, from ankle cuffs, I wondered, to join the chain between his wrists. It continued to the collar and then to the Master's hands. The Master was Mr Woods; the kneeling man beside him was Brian.

Self-discipline

I reached to put my arms round Brian for support as I burst into tears. He patted my back as I sobbed. I could feel our Speedos rubbing together. I held the photograph tight in my hands.

'Thank you,' Brian whispered.

I pulled back. I looked at him puzzled. I didn't understand.

'I thought I'd lost him,' he said.

The emotions hit me. I was jealous. I was scared. I was vulnerable, all at the same time. I wanted to be there, that man in the picture with Mr Woods. I was working towards sharing him with Peter, with Morgan. I hadn't allowed for sharing him with another, let alone Brian, in my calculations. I felt exposed. I hadn't invited Brian this far into my life, yet here he was, sharing my most intimate needs. He probably knew more about me now than I did myself. I felt scared. He held me as I sobbed.

It was a few minutes before I clenched my fists and gently pulled myself away from him. I handed him the picture frame. 'I don't understand,' I said. I wanted to ask so many questions. He put his arm round my shoulder and steered me towards our sitting room.

'I think we can put this here,' he said as he placed the photograph more openly on a bookshelf.

'Yes,' I said, 'that would be nice.'

'We can get another one soon.'

'Even better,' I said smiling.

I waited as Brian collected two glasses. I had to bite my lip to hold back more tears as he left the room. A moment later he was back, a bottle of wine and a corkscrew in his hands.

He didn't sit on the sofa, but on the floor in front of it, leaning back on it. He opened the wine as I sat down beside him. He poured wine into both glasses and handed one to me. He held his wine in one hand and reached for my spare hand with his. I let him hold me.

'Mr Woods,' he said, raising his glass.

'Mr Woods,' I said, accepting the toast.

We both savored the wine and the thought, and the bond as we held hands. I took a deep breath as I put my glass down. I looked at him directly. It was time for some explanations. He saw my expression.

'Don't worry,' he said, squeezing my hand. 'It's not that long a story.'

I took a sip of wine.

'I know Mr Woods, how shall I say, "of old",' he began. 'Well, at least of a few years ago. We met when I was working in the States. I was living with a guy called George. I was trying to be his slave, his houseboy, but it wasn't really working. I'd come home from work and find that he'd got away early, that he'd done the dishes, cleaned house, swept the yard, fixed dinner. There was nothing left for me to do. The play was good, but, you know, it was almost as if he was a slave too, trying to be something that he really wasn't.

'It took me a while to realize what was happening, that our body and mind timetables weren't working together. We were horny at different times. It wasn't working. He was a nice enough guy. We'd had fun, especially at the beginning. I'd learned a lot from him, especially how to behave, and about my own body, what it would take and what I could enjoy from it. He'd helped me learn to relax, to appreciate the intensity of stimulation without being distracted by notions of pain. He had helped me discover the true joy of placing my body in another man's hands. He'd introduced me to skilled players, to some of the most accomplished tops. He'd stroked my face, kissed me, held my hands when I'd been whipped for the very first time. He'd played with me, kept me on the edge of orgasm while I'd been flogged. Without me realizing it, he'd conditioned me so that my upper back became one of my most erogenous zones. 'His request had come as something of a surprise. One evening when I came in from work he told me that he'd met an old friend, a physician who was in town for a conference. He'd invited him for dinner the next day. Sure, I'd said, where were we going? We rarely had anyone to our home.

'He was coming here, I was told, and that I would be serving dinner. I needn't worry about cooking, he'd order in, but I'd have to wait table. He didn't need to say anything. I knew the guy was something special. I felt George was trying to prove something. I wasn't sure what. There was one other thing, George said, this guy liked Speedos. That would be all I would wear.

'I didn't say anything. There was something from George's attitude that told me this guy was special. Sure, I told George,

I'd do it, no problem, but it wasn't for him, it was for this unknown guy. There was something about George, a nervousness I thought, that I noticed.

'The idea excited me. I remember that I didn't sleep much that night. I was making plans. I was up early the next day. George was still sleeping as I used the shower. I shaved myself more than I had ever done before, from the neck to between my legs. I shaved the crack of my ass too. I ran to the gym, taking my work clothes with me. I worked out more determinedly than I'd done in weeks. I wondered what was happening to me as I worked that morning.

What was it that was making put so much effort into impressing someone I'd never met? Someone I knew almost nothing about?

'I got away as early as I could for lunch and headed for the stores. I had Speedos at home, for sure, but I wanted something special for this guy. It took me a while, but I found them. I wanted a light color, something that would not hide the shadows; the outline of my cock and balls would look better if there were shadows. I wanted something high cut and reasonably tight.

'I was tempted to wear them that afternoon at work, but I didn't. I wanted them to be fresh and new for this mysterious guest.

'I stopped off going home to buy flowers for the table. George would never have thought of flowers. I bought candles too. I called by the local store and bought fresh herbs too.

'When I got home, I took over. George hadn't seen me like that for a while. I put the different dishes into the right bowls. I polished and set the dining table for two. I picked two wines from our stock. I polished the glasses. I banished George from the dining area and kitchen. If you want me to do this, I'd told him, I'm going to do it properly. It was far too petulant. If he was really a Master, my Master, he would have punished me. It was opening my door.

'Our guest was due at seven. At 6.30, I went and showered. I ran the razor over my chest and stomach again, just to make sure. I dried myself carefully. I pulled on a cock ring. I took the brand new Speedos from their bag. I kissed them before putting them on. I didn't know why. I just knew I wanted to impress this guy. There was a chance, I didn't know what of, I just knew there was something.

'George didn't even notice that I'd shaved my body. He moved towards the door when the bell rang. I looked daggers at him as he got up and started to go to open it. If you want me to be a slave for the evening, let me be a slave, I thought. Don't cramp my style.

'I opened the door and held it back so George could welcome his guest. I was glad I was at one side, out of his direct line of sight, when Mr Woods came in. I gasped. There was something about the man. I felt my cock react in my Speedos. For a moment, I wished they weren't quite as tight. My erection would be exceedingly obvious.

'But Mr Woods is so polite and courteous. There was no sign that he had noticed my appearance. He thanked me as I served them wine and then dinner. He was wearing a business suit but filled it well. I felt his presence. George did too. He was very nervous. He looked uncomfortable sitting at the same table. I must admit that I enjoyed watching that. It made me feel more at ease. George was almost incidental. I was doing it for Mr Woods, and enjoying it.

'I'd served them brandy on the deck after dinner. I called Mr Woods a cab when he said he was ready to leave. I hadn't noticed him do it, but when I was holding the door open for him to go, he handed me a business card. I'd bowed, said 'thank you, Sir' and closed the door behind me before looking at it. George had already retreated to the kitchen and was clearing up. I went to put the card in my note book, where it would be safe. I didn't notice the writing on the back until then. There were just a few words. The name of a prestigious downtown hotel, the time – 6pm – and "be there". I knew I would.'

Brian's story sounded familiar. Mr Woods' modus operandi had been very much the same for Peter, I recalled.

'And,' I said, 'At six o'clock the next day, there you were, waiting in the lobby of the hotel.'

'That's not quite the end of my story,' Brian said. 'I started seeing Mr Woods regularly when he was in the city. He was there for two or three days a month on business for about a year. My relationship with George changed. I moved into the spare room. We became roommates. George didn't want to know about my time away, when I was with Mr Woods. He'd ask about him, every so often, in a distant sort of way. It was almost as if he was afraid of himself.'

I nodded.

'Then, I had a chance of a new job. It was a promotion. I moved, to a new city. I had new friends. I changed for a while. George had tried to be a master, I did too. I was a demanding, impatient boss. I must have been hell to work for. It felt good, this perception of power, but I didn't like myself for it.

'I rebelled. I tried to repress the slave within. It worked, for a while. I threw Mr Woods' details away. I didn't want to know. That was past. It was a part of me that I thought I'd lived through. A phase. I wondered if being gay was the same. I even dated a couple of women. That didn't feel right.

'I could be gay, but I didn't need to be a slave. That was the deal I did with myself. I went to the bars. I picked up some nice guys, most with good bodies, some with good minds too. I made some good money. The company liked me, but, as the months went passed and the balance in my account grew, I became more and more aware that something was missing from my life, something important, very important.

'Then, suddenly, that life was no more. One day, I was working my way to the executive floor, taking calls from analysts and brokers, reading reports from development managers and project executives. The next I had no job, no security pass, no ID. There was a stack of cash in my account, insurances paid in advance for two years. The company had been bought out, taken over, just like that. Sure, there had been some rumors, but nothing too serious. Everyone had thought we'd be the company doing the buying. Then, suddenly, it wasn't like that any more. We were the ones who were swallowed. They closed our office. Those who were staying were moved, within days. The rest of us, we were out.

'I enjoyed the break. I traveled some. I sought sun to overcome the shock. I tidied my résumé. I contacted the headhunters, the agencies. I wrote to old friends, past contacts, old enemies. That's why I'm here. One responded. He'd had the same experience of sudden redundancy, he said in his letter. It had affected him badly, but after the initial shock and depression, he'd fought his way back. He couldn't offer me much, he said, but he remembered my work, my determination. Six months, he'd said, perhaps a year at the most, to prove myself. I'd accepted. I was on a plane within days. I stayed with friends, used a hotel a few nights, until I saw your listing.'

'And Mr Woods?' I asked.

'Your letter,' said Brian, sighing. 'The one you showed me last week. I recognized the handwriting immediately. I should have said something.'

'You didn't have to,' I said, reaching for his hand.

'I wrote the following day. It was a long letter.'

'I can imagine,' I said.

'He recognized this address. He called me last week. I'm sorry, Jimmy, but I didn't feel I could say anything then.'

'And now?'

'And now you know.'

'Everything?'

'Almost.'

I looked at him. I didn't want to ask. I wanted him to tell me because he wanted to.

'A parcel arrived on Saturday morning. I was still asleep when the mail arrived. The bell was ringing for ages before I staggered to the door. The mailman was about to leave when I finally got there.'

'And?' I said.

Brian stood up. He pulled me to my feet and guided me back into his room.

There, on his wardrobe, was a small collection of garments – a boxer brief, another Speedo, two thongs and a jockstrap.

'I hope you don't mind, too much,' he said, 'but I'm coming with you on Friday.'

THE END

About the author

Chris Charlton is in his fifties and has been interested in power relationships and SM for more nearly forty years. He is a professional writer and journalist, covering health, including HIV, and the media. He takes his play and relationships seriously, being a long-standing member of one of the leading SM clubs in the US. He read psychology at university in England.

Taking inspiration from leading writers such as John Preston, Race Bannon, Joseph Bean and Guy Baldwin, Chris Charlton looks for the beautiful, the positive and the inspirational in the honesty that allows people to appreciate the power dynamics of dominance and willing submission.

Chris's interests include many aspects of physical SM, the exploration of the body and its responses. He is also intrigued by the ways in which finding and being open about the power dynamics between people can keep the most intimate relationships alive and exciting.

Revelation is the first in a series of stories exploring domestic power relationships and the minds of those attracted to them.

You can write to Chris at chrschlrtn@gmail.com